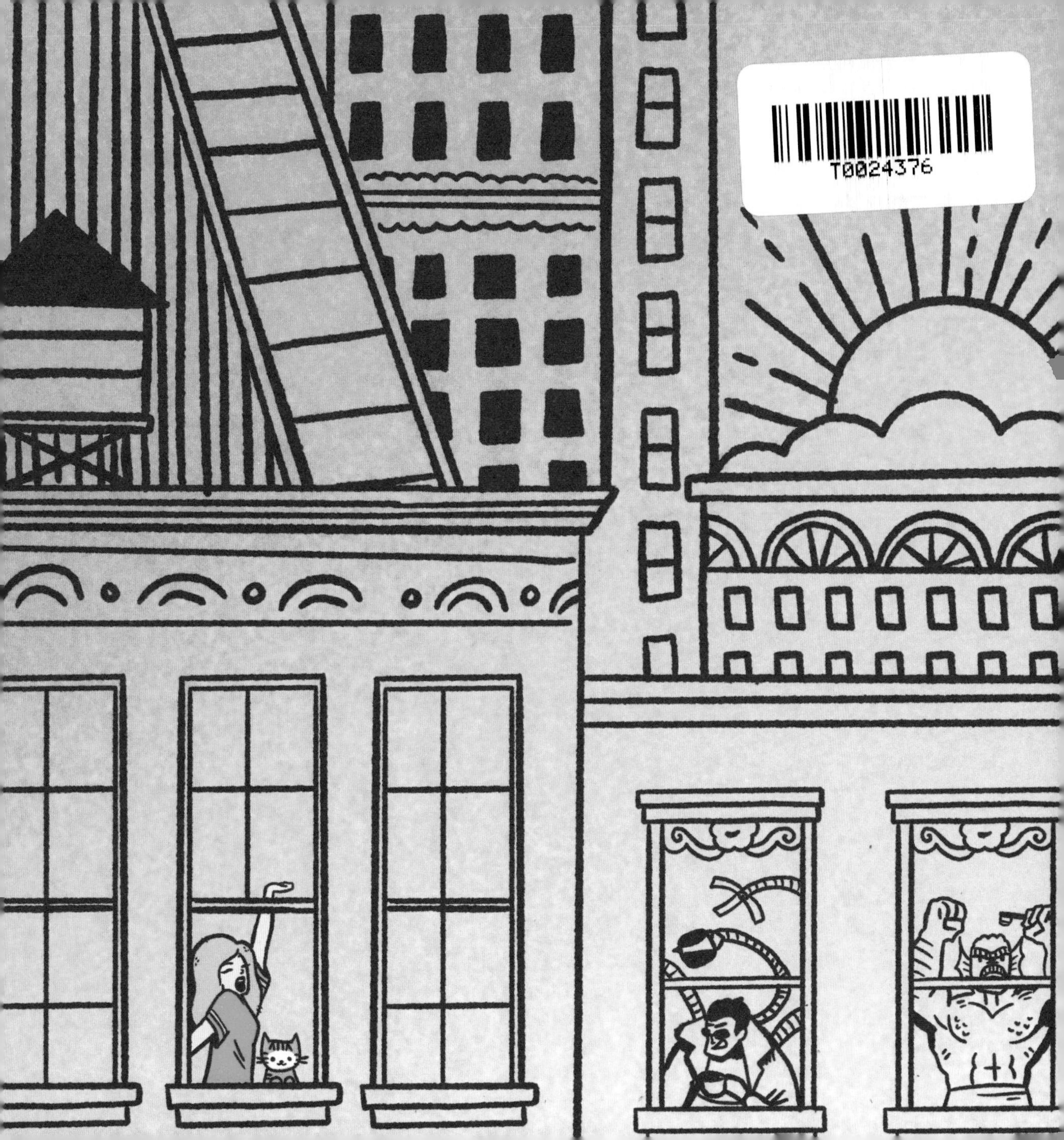

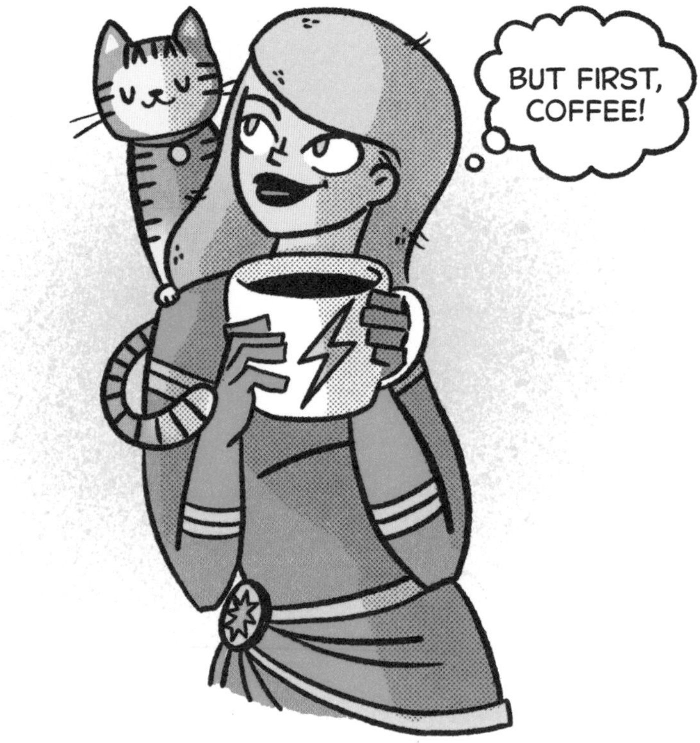
BUT FIRST, COFFEE!

MARVEL

HELLO HEROES

CAPTAIN MARVEL SOARS ABOVE

Abrams Books for Young Readers
New York

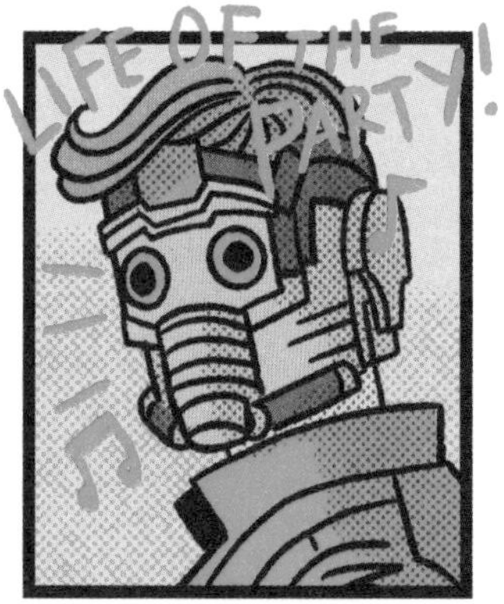
LIFE OF THE PARTY!

STAR-LORD

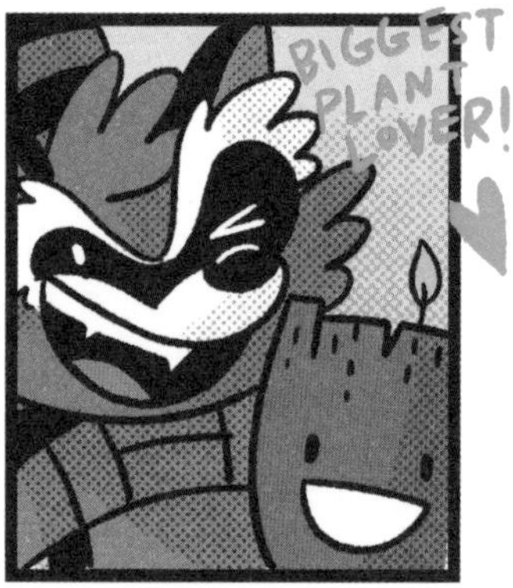
BIGGEST PLANT LOVER!

ROCKET & GROOT

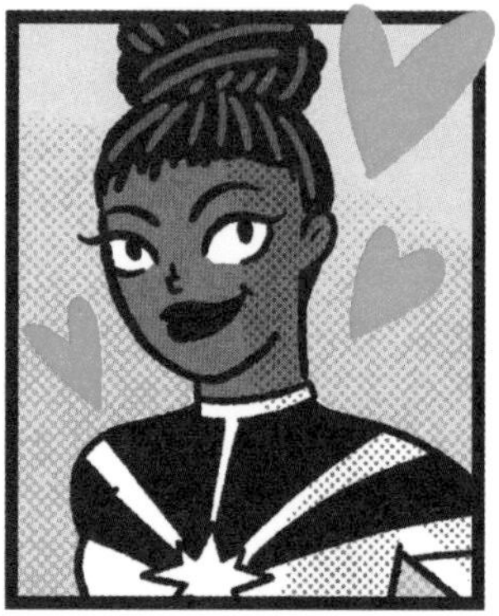

MONICA RAMBEAU

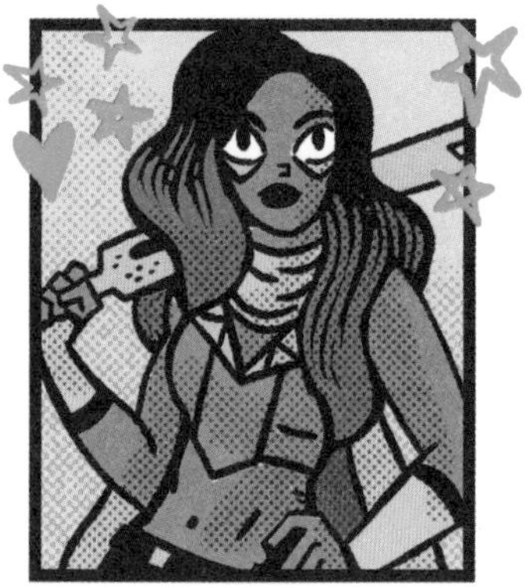

GAMORA

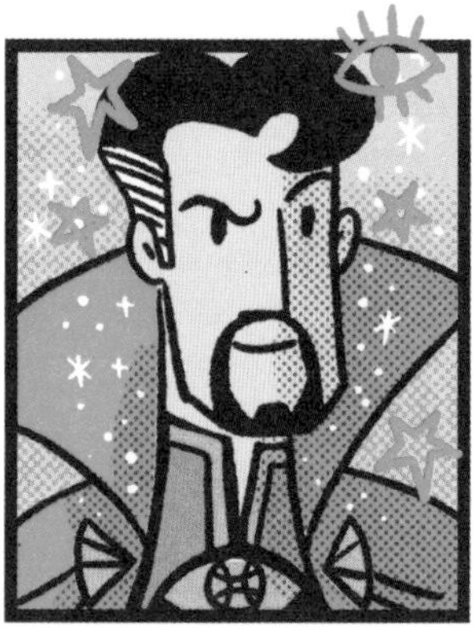

DOCTOR STRANGE

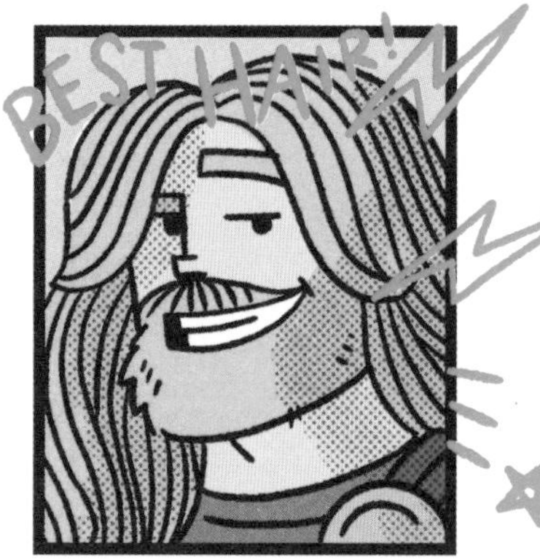
BEST HAIR!

THOR

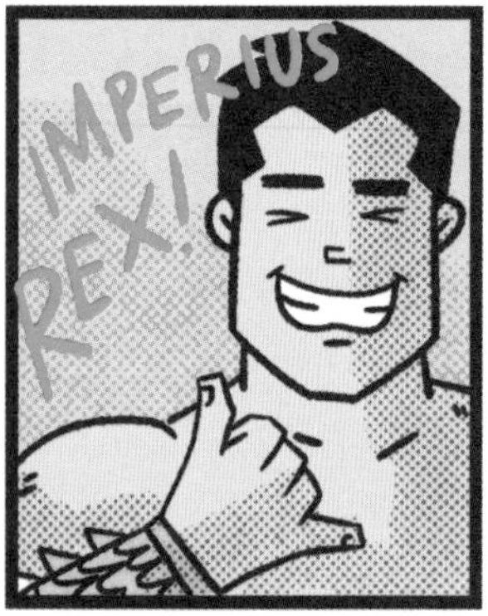
IMPERIUS REX!

NAMOR

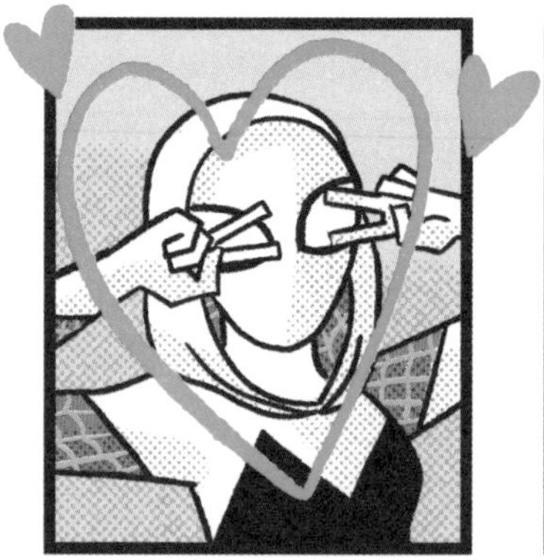

GHOST-SPIDER

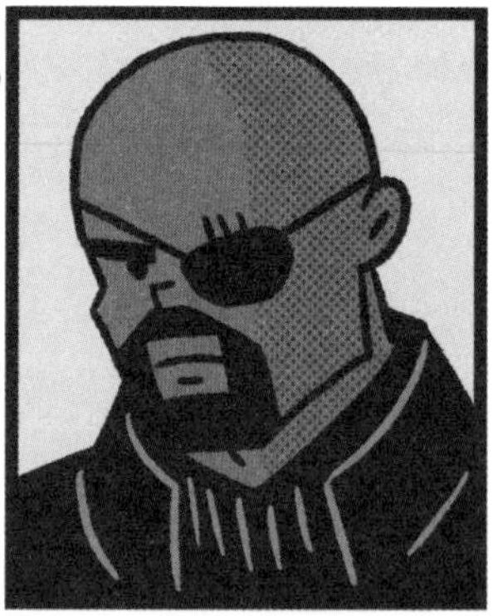

NICK FURY

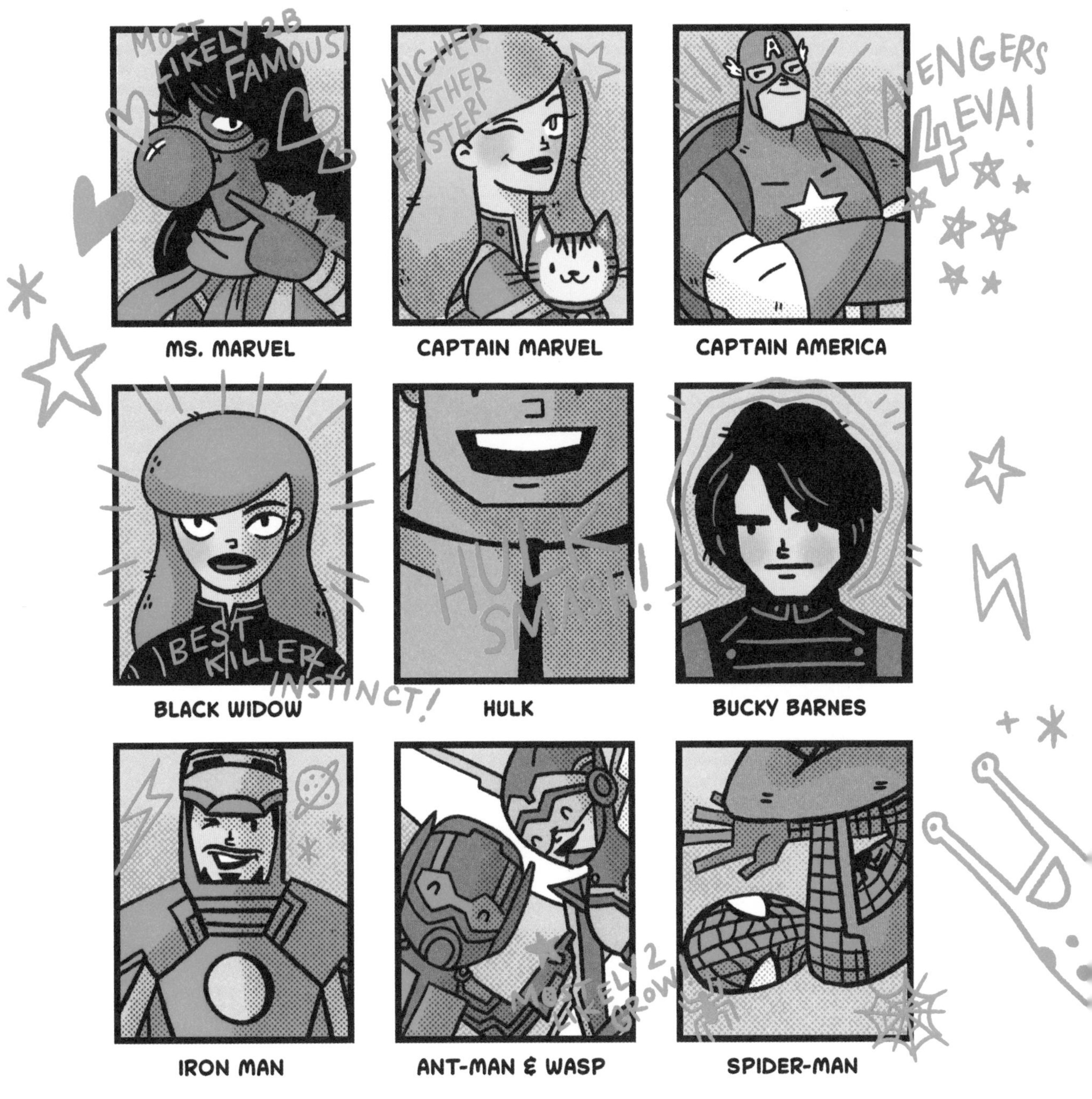
MOST LIKELY 2B FAMOUS!
MS. MARVEL
HIGHER FURTHER FASTER!
CAPTAIN MARVEL
AVENGERS 4EVA!
CAPTAIN AMERICA
BEST KILLER INSTINCT!
BLACK WIDOW
HULK SMASH!
HULK
BUCKY BARNES
IRON MAN
MOST LIKELY 2 GROW
ANT-MAN & WASP
SPIDER-MAN

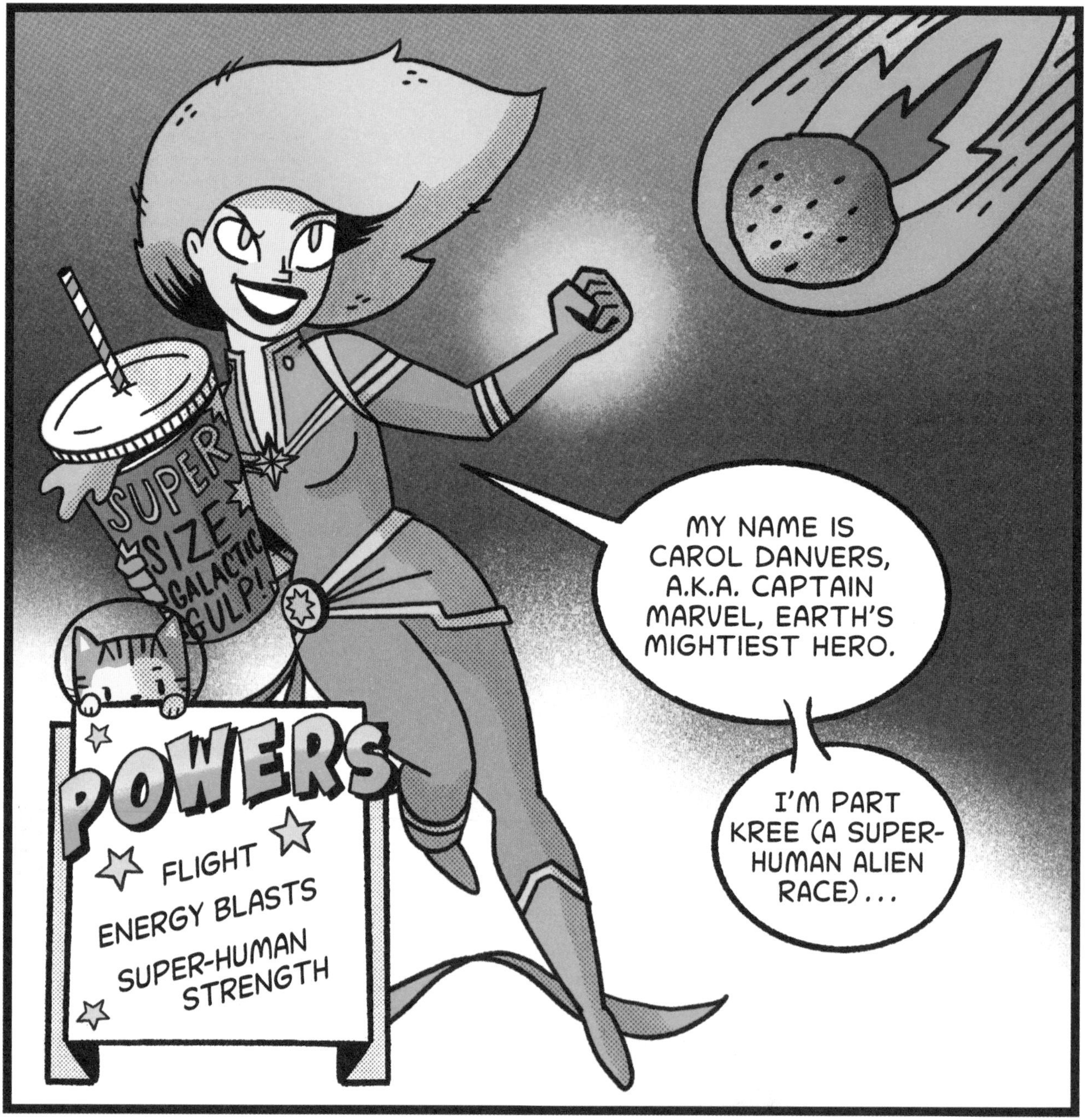

SUPER SIZE GALACTIC GULP!
POWERS
FLIGHT
ENERGY BLASTS
SUPER-HUMAN STRENGTH
MY NAME IS CAROL DANVERS, A.K.A. CAPTAIN MARVEL, EARTH'S MIGHTIEST HERO.
I'M PART KREE (A SUPER-HUMAN ALIEN RACE)...

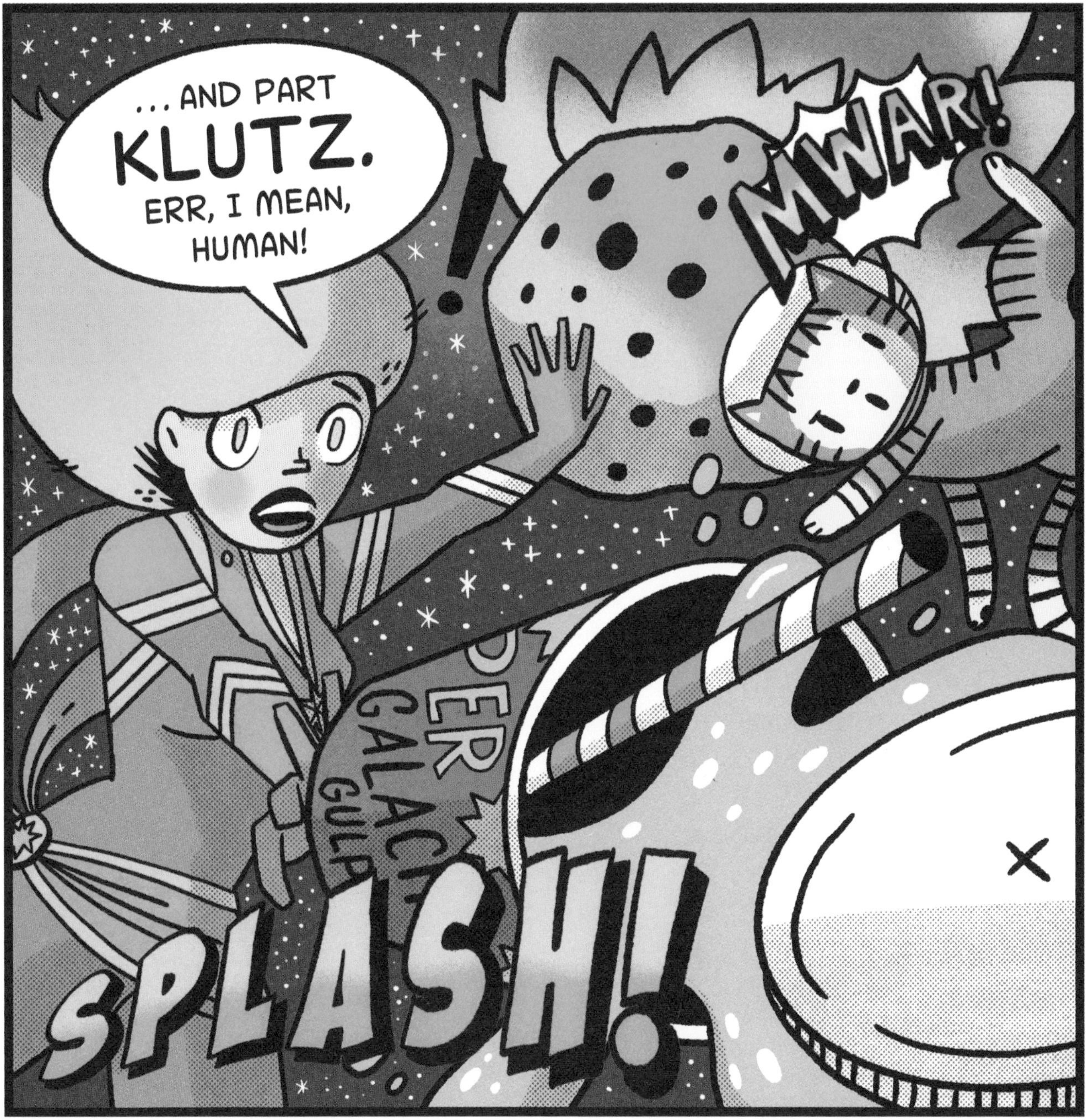

... AND PART KLUTZ. ERR, I MEAN, HUMAN!
!
MWAR!
SPLASH!

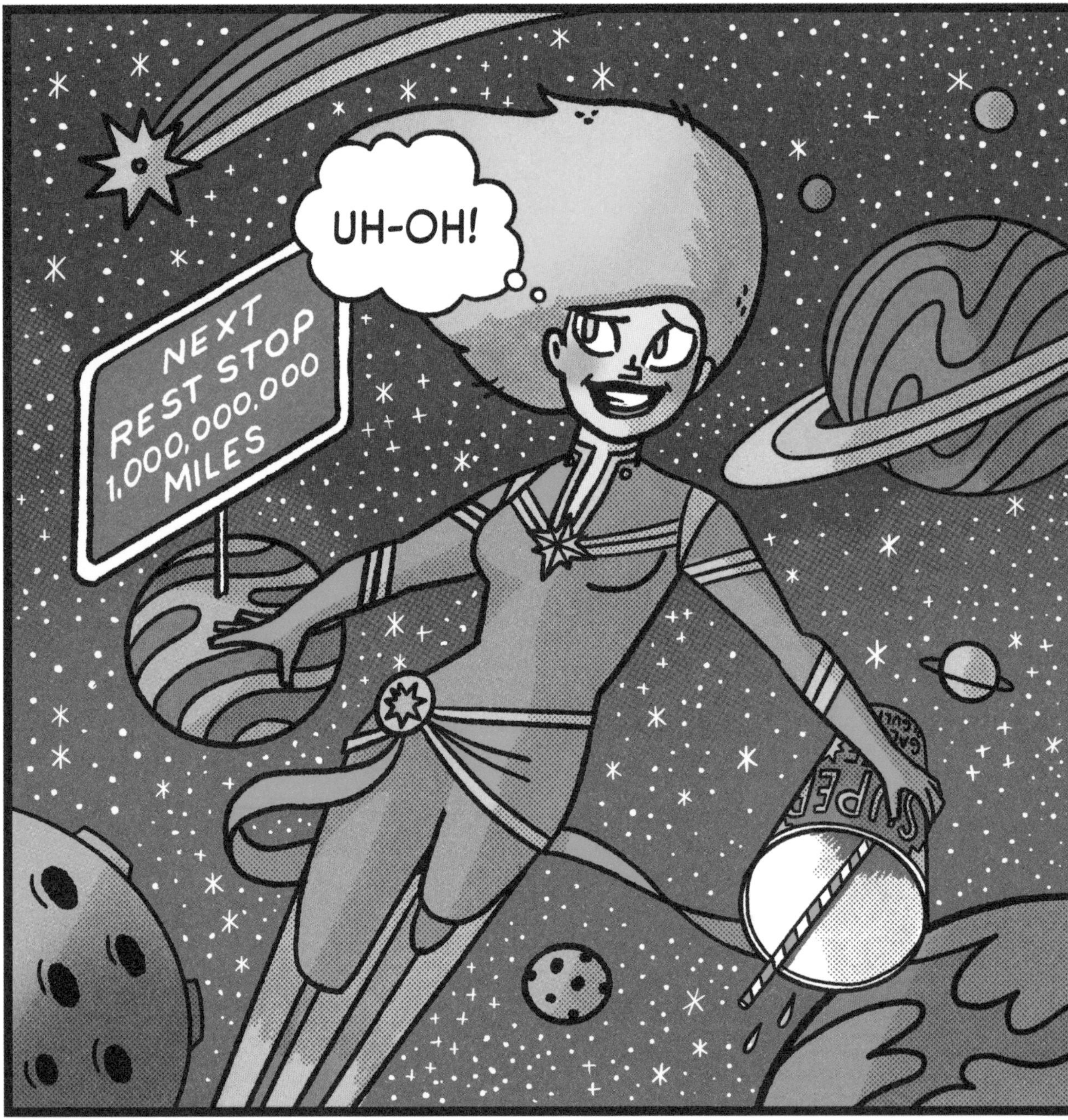
UH-OH!
NEXT
REST STOP
1,000,000,000
MILES

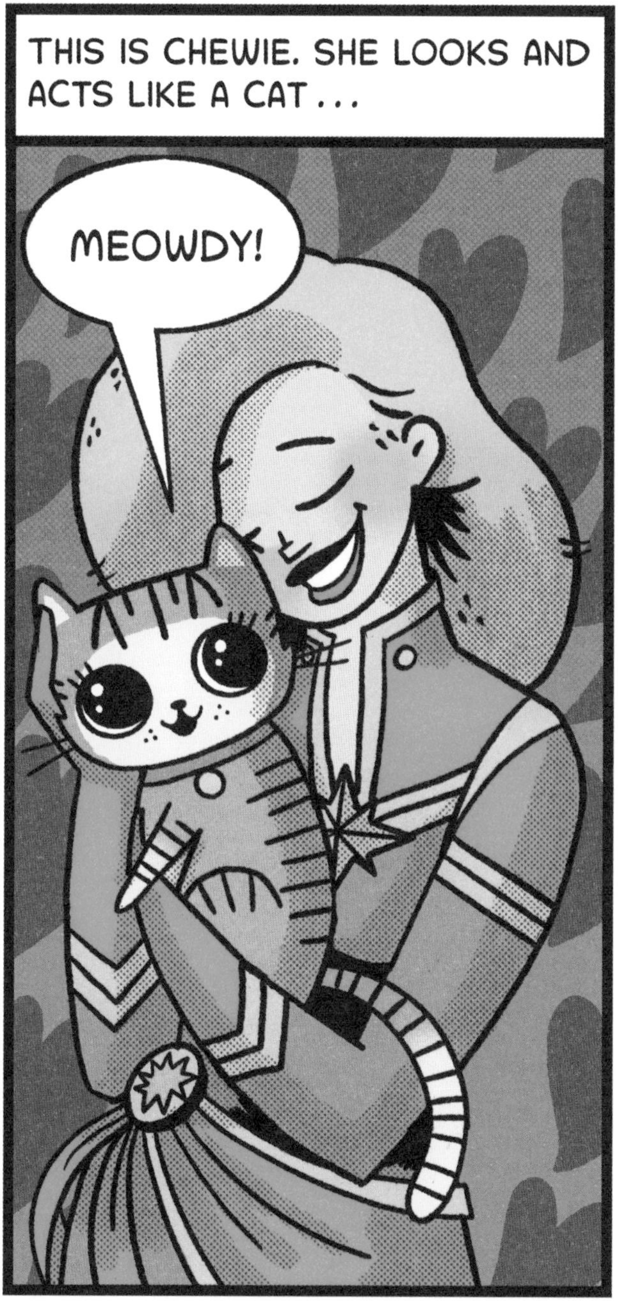
THIS IS CHEWIE. SHE LOOKS AND ACTS LIKE A CAT . . .
MEOWDY!

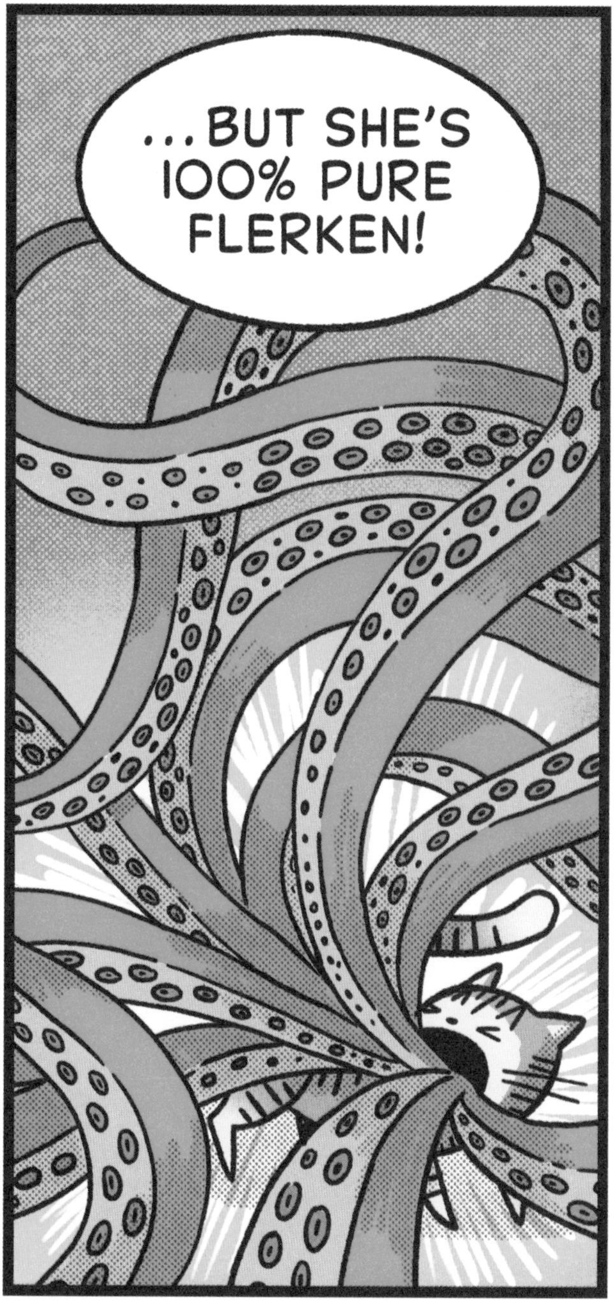
. . . BUT SHE'S 100% PURE FLERKEN!

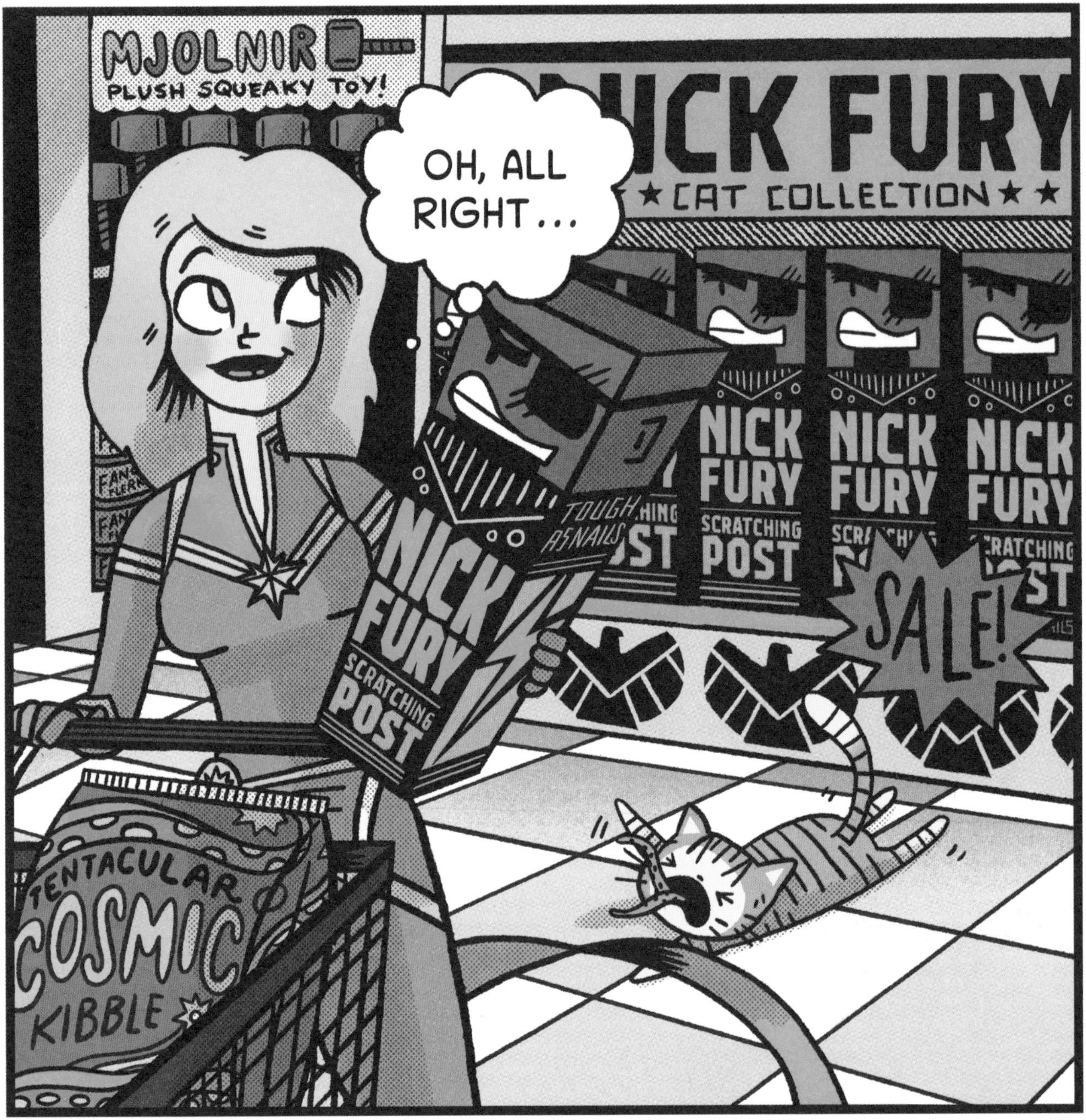

MJOLNIR
PLUSH SQUEAKY TOY!
★ CAT COLLECTION ★ ★
OH, ALL RIGHT...
NICK FURY
SCRATCHING POST
TOUGH AS NAILS
SALE!
TENTACULAR
COSMIC
KIBBLE

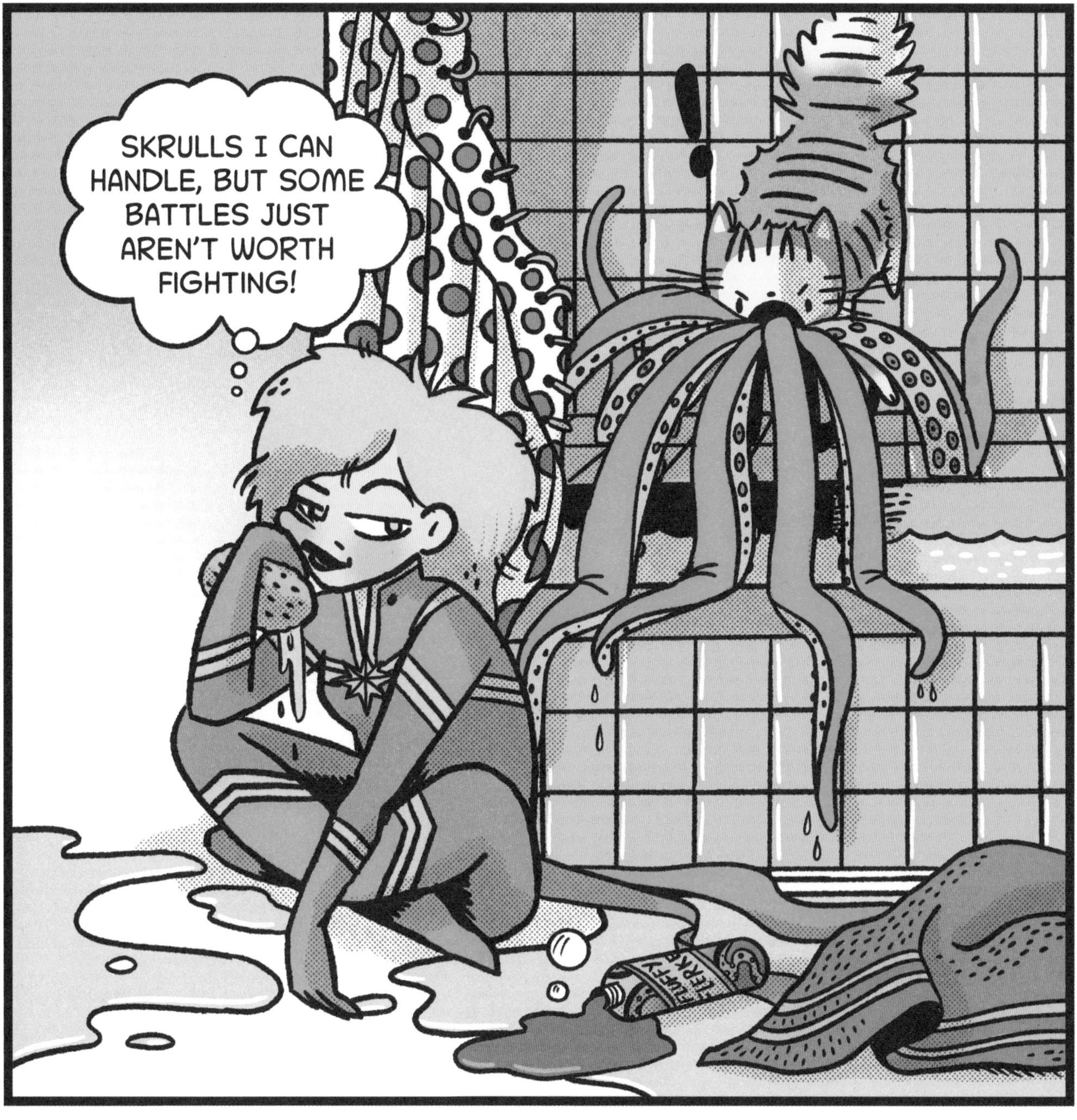
SKRULLS I CAN HANDLE, BUT SOME BATTLES JUST AREN'T WORTH FIGHTING!

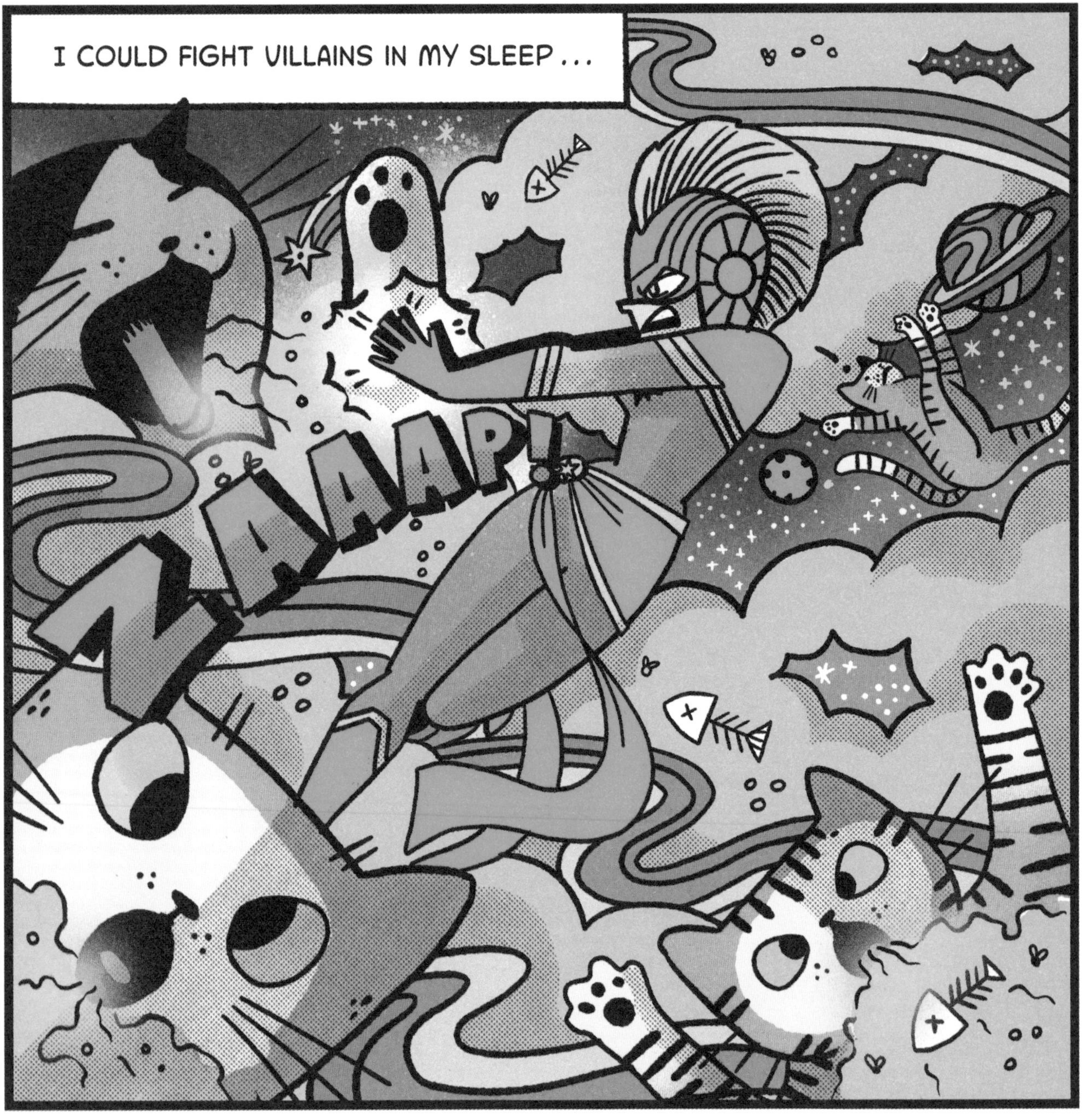
I COULD FIGHT VILLAINS IN MY SLEEP . . .
ZAAAP!

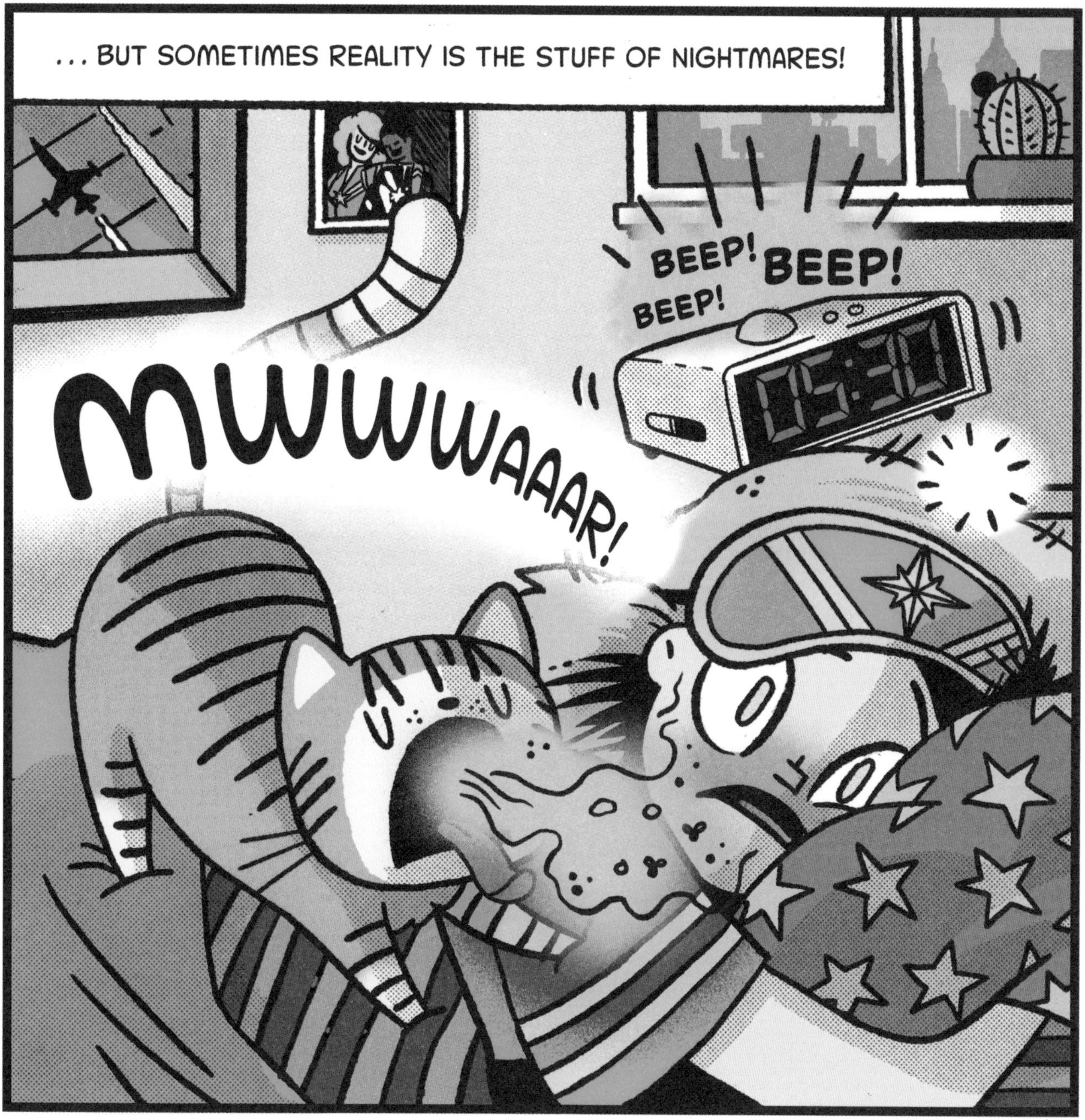
. . . BUT SOMETIMES REALITY IS THE STUFF OF NIGHTMARES!
BEEP!
BEEP!
BEEP!
05:30
MWWWAAAR!

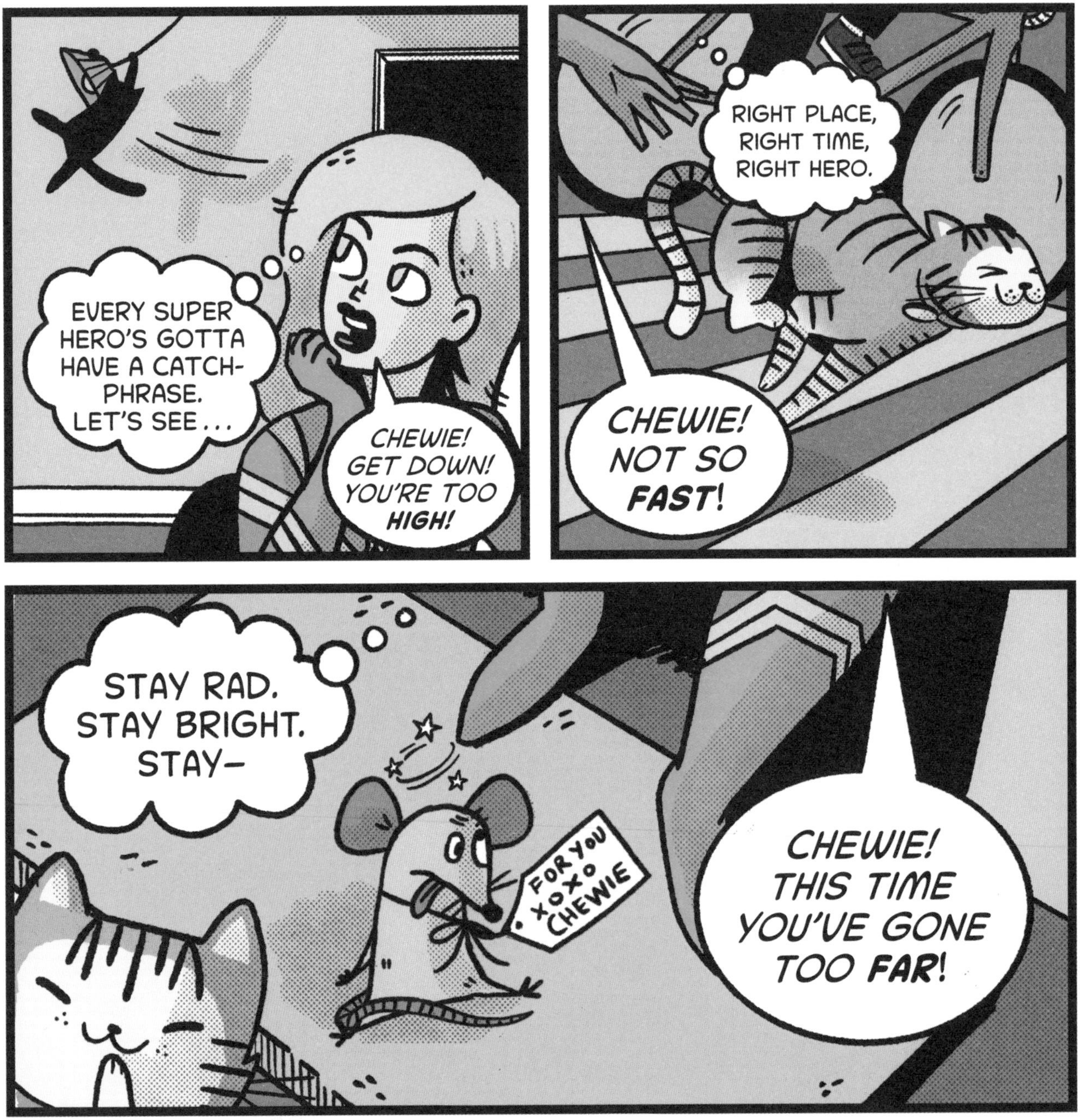
EVERY SUPER HERO'S GOTTA HAVE A CATCH-PHRASE. LET'S SEE . . .
CHEWIE! GET DOWN! YOU'RE TOO HIGH!
RIGHT PLACE, RIGHT TIME, RIGHT HERO.
CHEWIE! NOT SO FAST!
STAY RAD. STAY BRIGHT. STAY–
FOR YOU XOXO CHEWIE
CHEWIE! THIS TIME YOU'VE GONE TOO FAR!

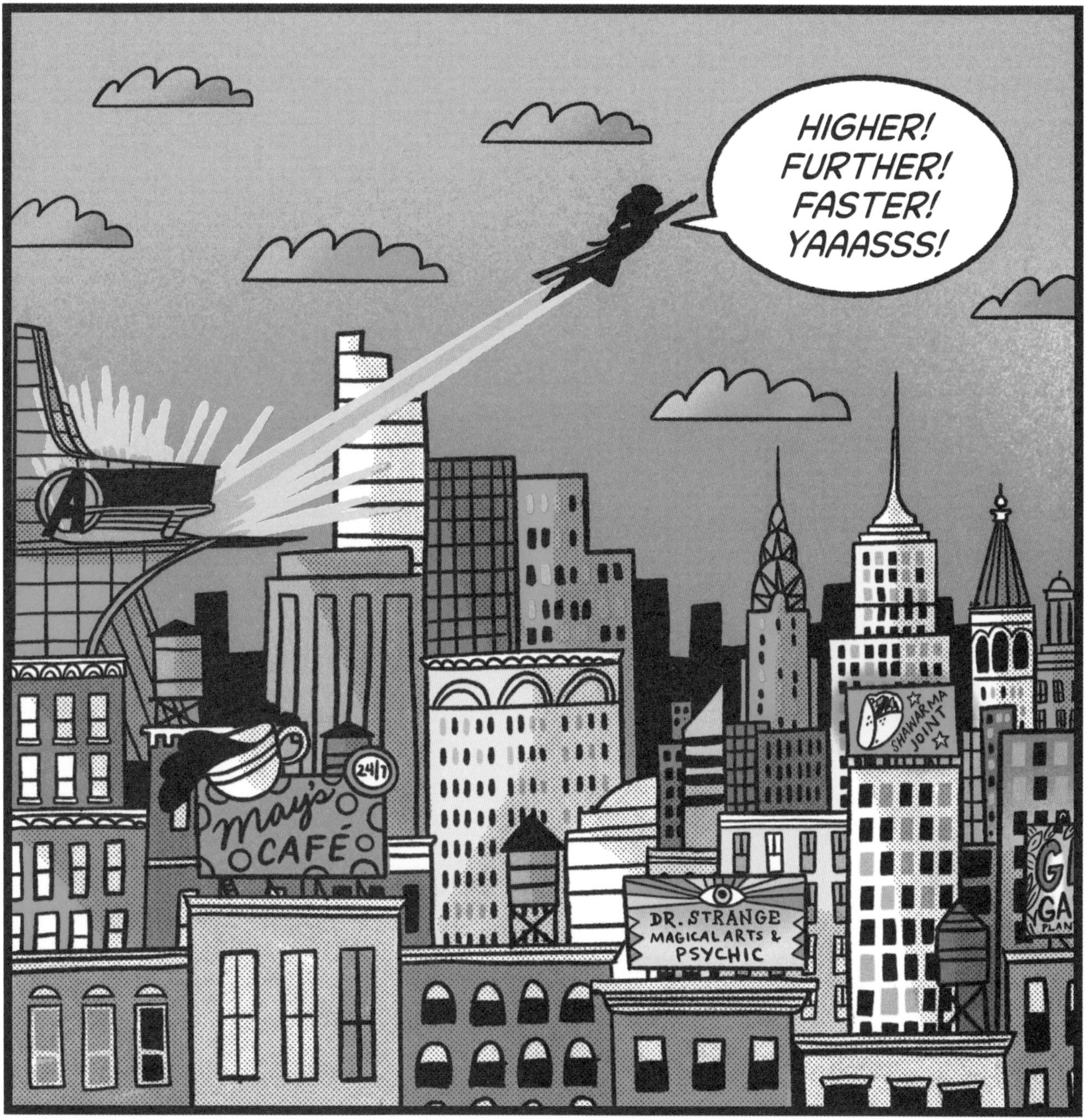
HIGHER! FURTHER! FASTER! YAAASSS!
May's CAFÉ
24/7
SHAWARMA JOINT
DR. STRANGE MAGICAL ARTS & PSYCHIC

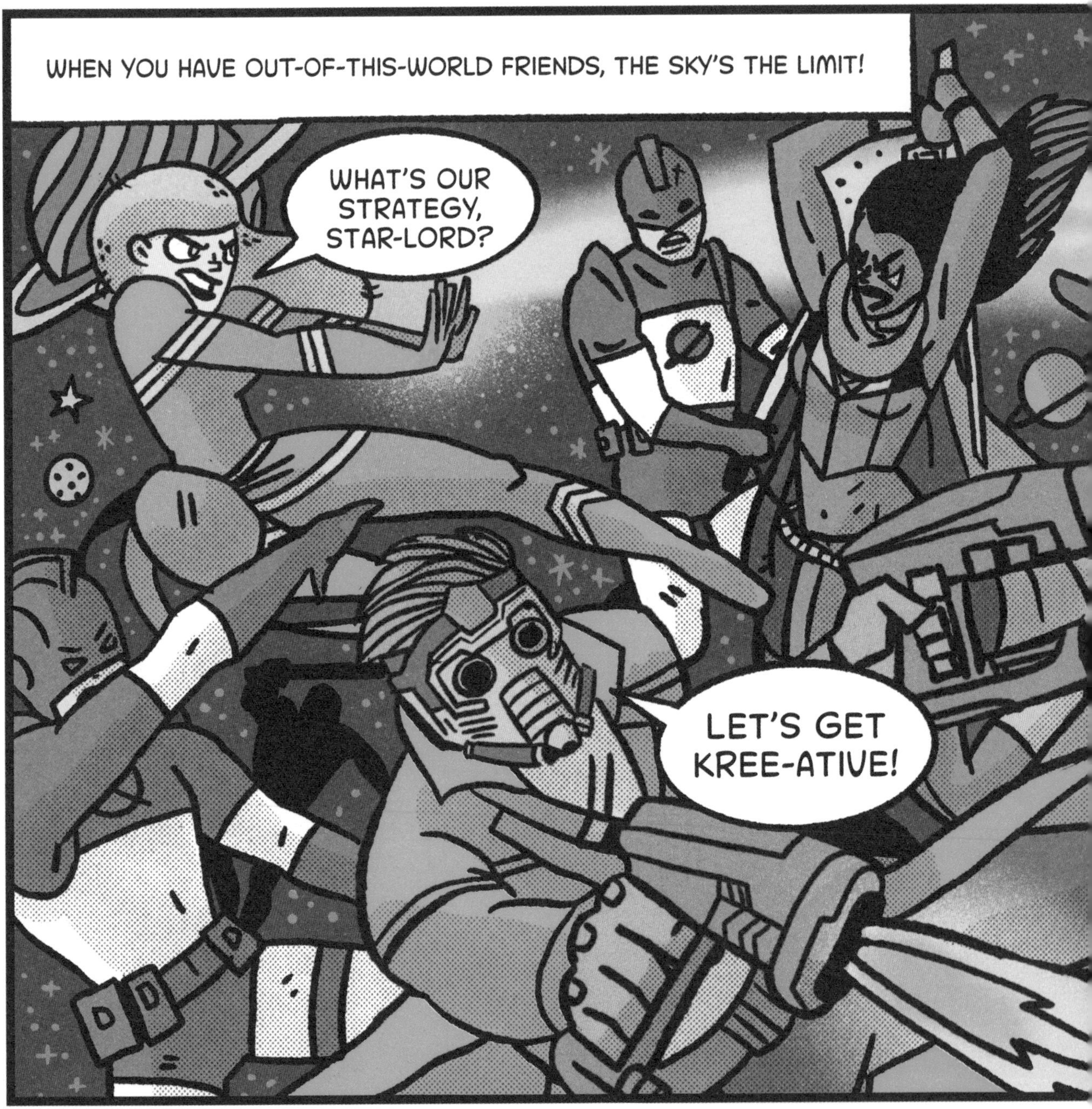
WHEN YOU HAVE OUT-OF-THIS-WORLD FRIENDS, THE SKY'S THE LIMIT!
WHAT'S OUR STRATEGY, STAR-LORD?
LET'S GET KREE-ATIVE!

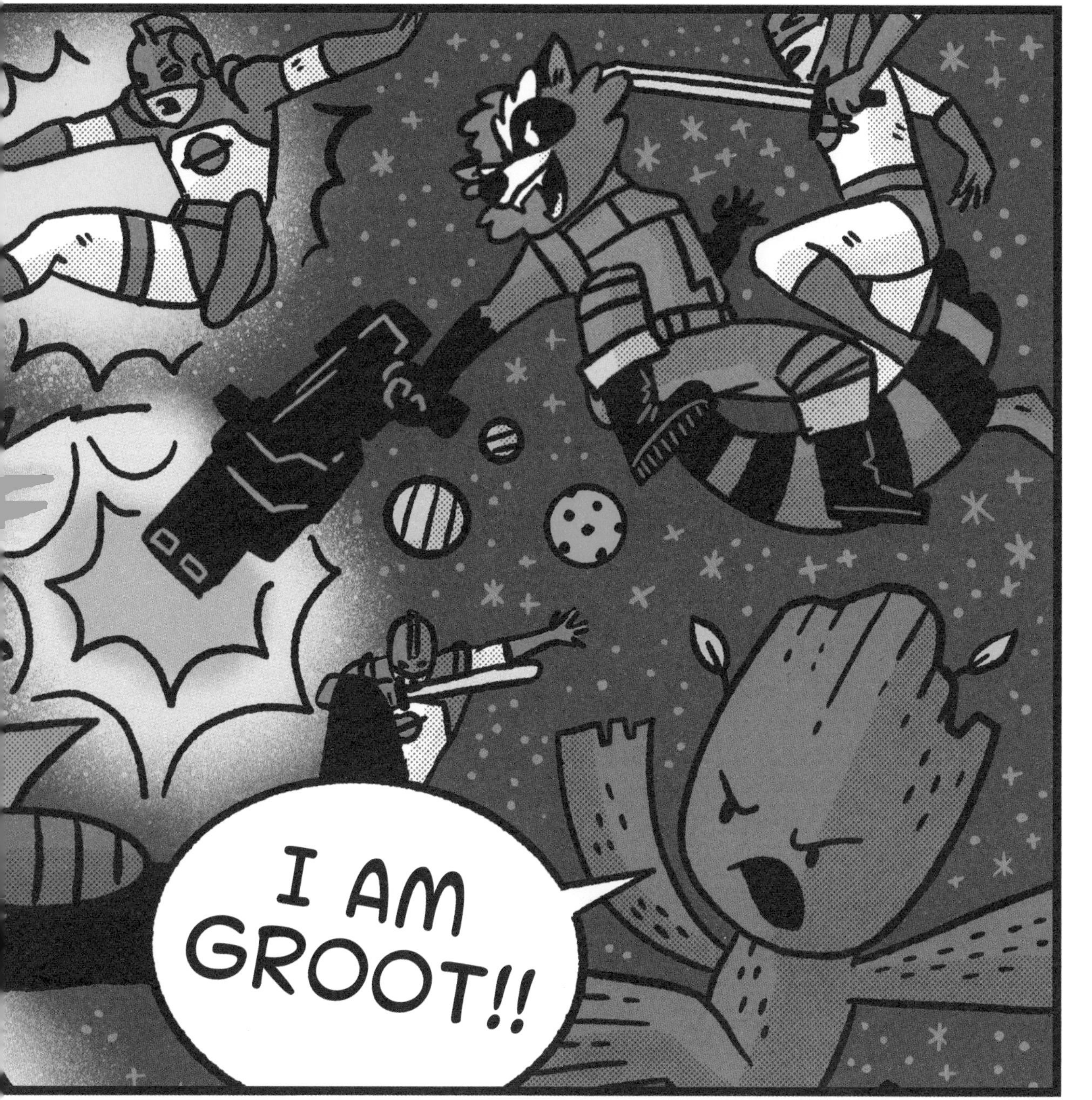
I AM GROOT!!

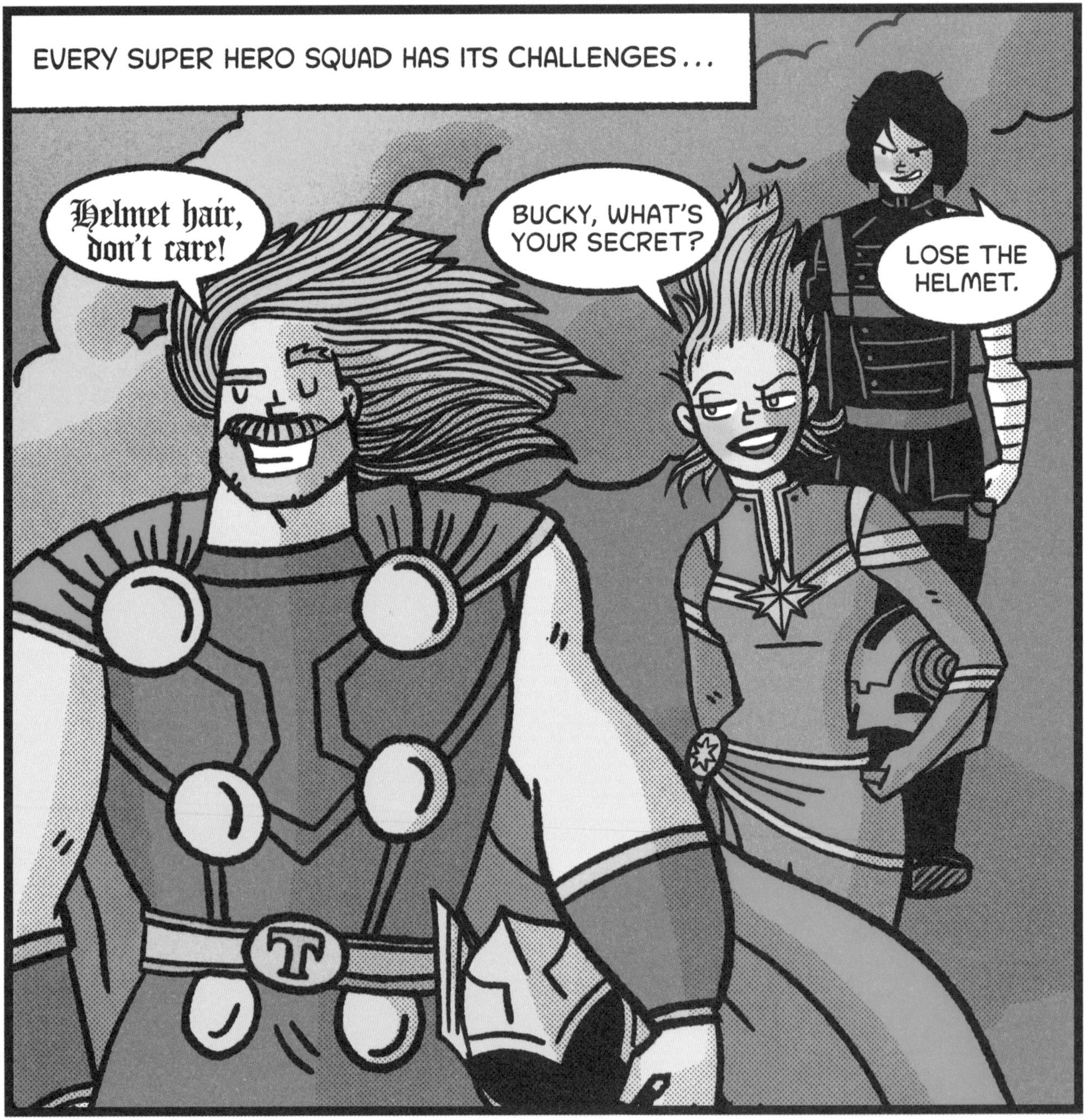

EVERY SUPER HERO SQUAD HAS ITS CHALLENGES...
Helmet hair, don't care!
BUCKY, WHAT'S YOUR SECRET?
LOSE THE HELMET.

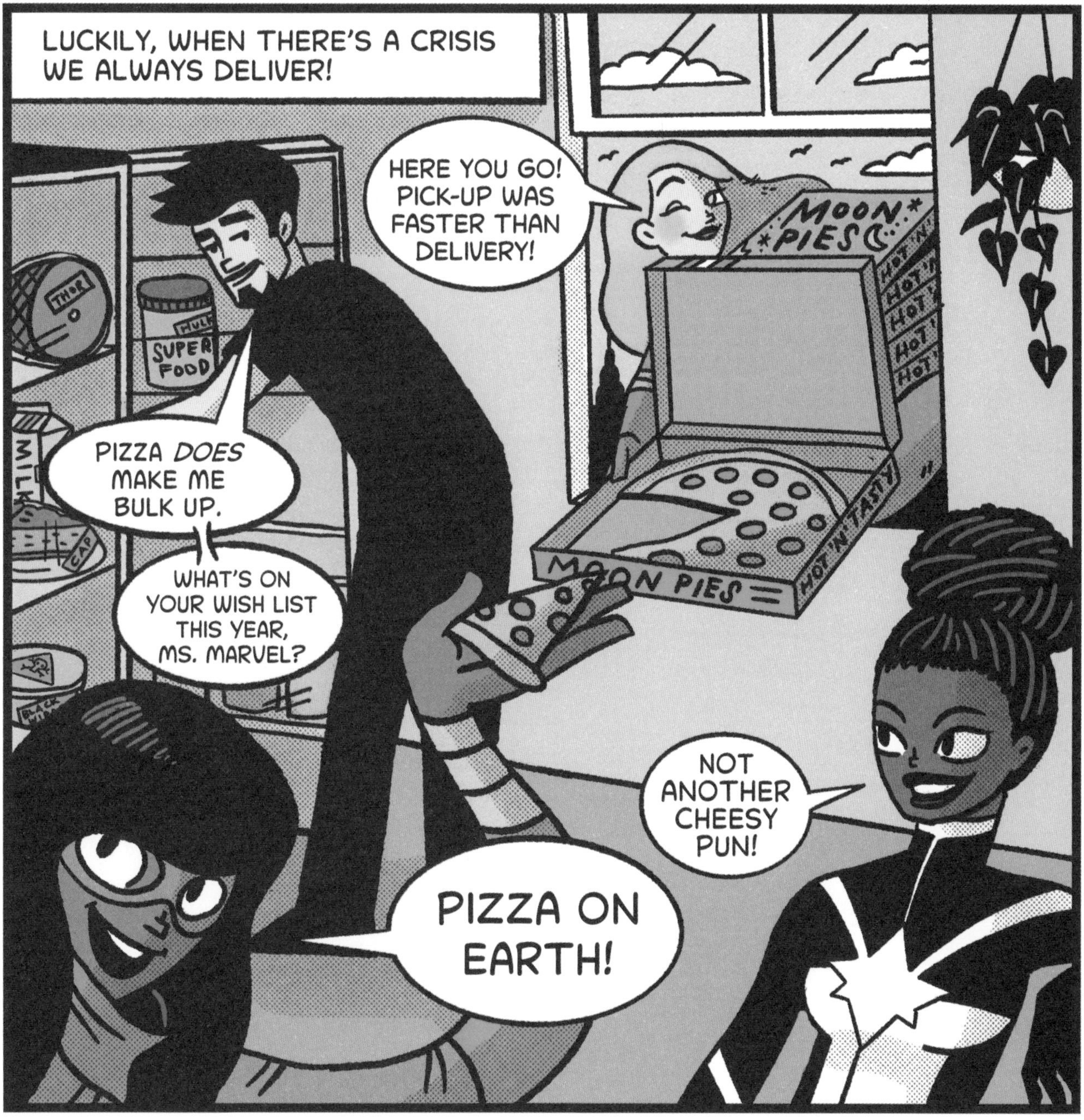
LUCKILY, WHEN THERE'S A CRISIS WE ALWAYS DELIVER!
HERE YOU GO! PICK-UP WAS FASTER THAN DELIVERY!
MOON PIES
HOT 'N' TASTY
THOR
HULK
SUPER FOOD
MILK
CAP
PIZZA *DOES* MAKE ME BULK UP.
WHAT'S ON YOUR WISH LIST THIS YEAR, MS. MARVEL?
MOON PIES
NOT ANOTHER CHEESY PUN!
PIZZA ON EARTH!

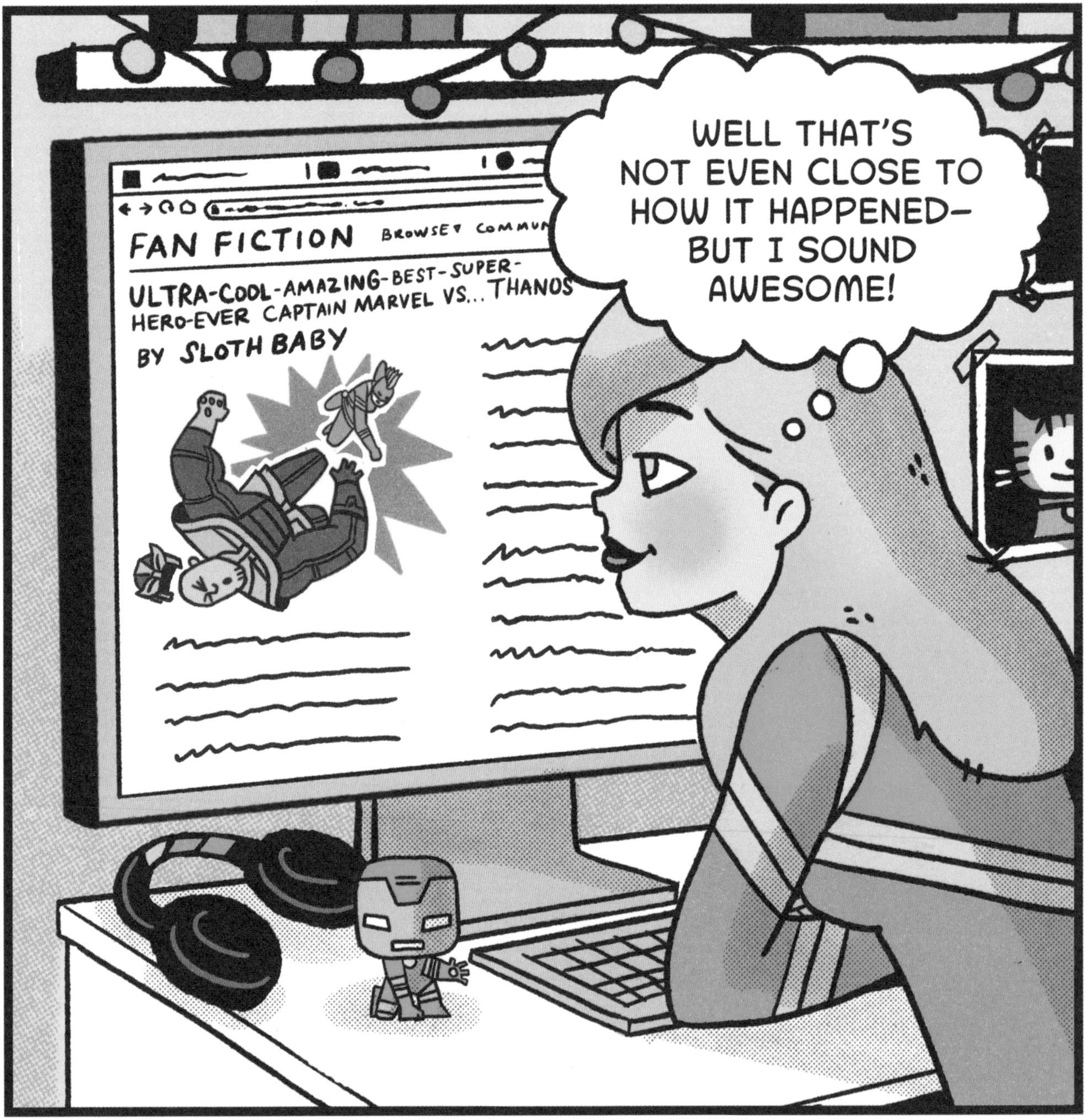

FAN FICTION
BROWSE COMMUN
ULTRA-COOL-AMAZING-BEST-SUPER-HERO-EVER CAPTAIN MARVEL VS... THANOS
BY SLOTH BABY
WELL THAT'S NOT EVEN CLOSE TO HOW IT HAPPENED— BUT I SOUND AWESOME!

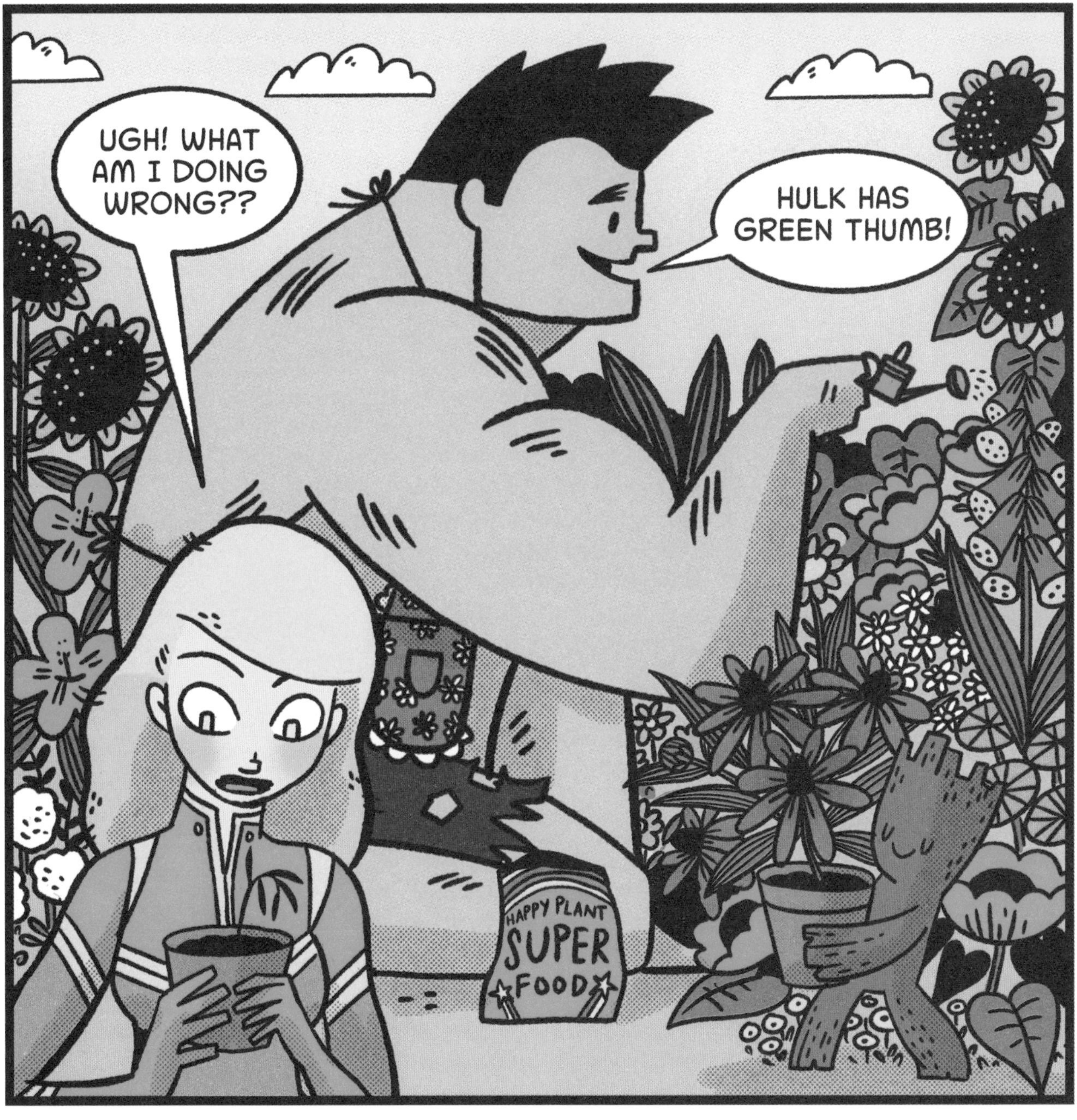
UGH! WHAT AM I DOING WRONG??
HULK HAS GREEN THUMB!
HAPPY PLANT SUPER FOOD

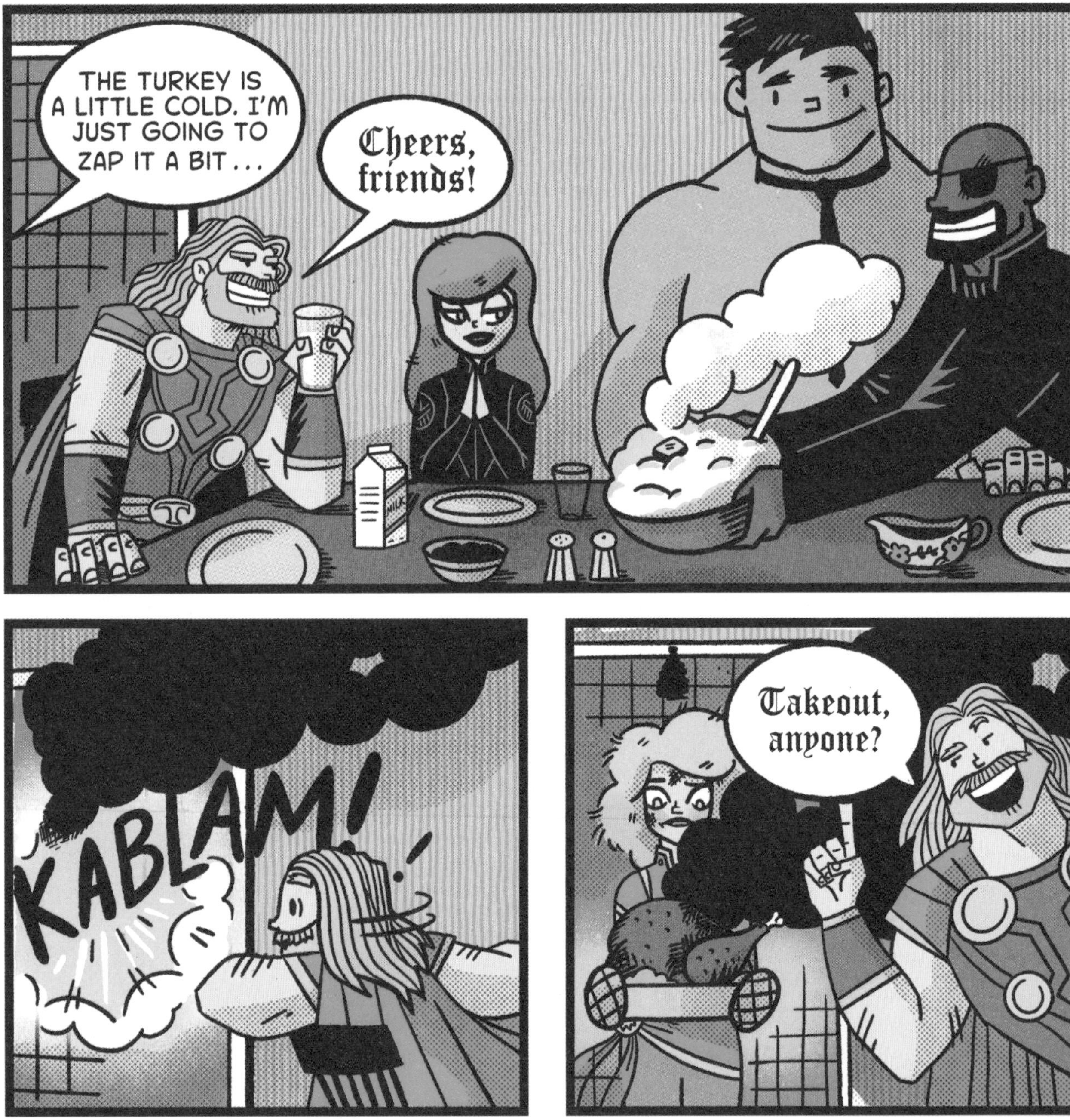
THE TURKEY IS A LITTLE COLD. I'M JUST GOING TO ZAP IT A BIT . . .
Cheers, friends!
MILK
KABLAM!
Takeout, anyone?

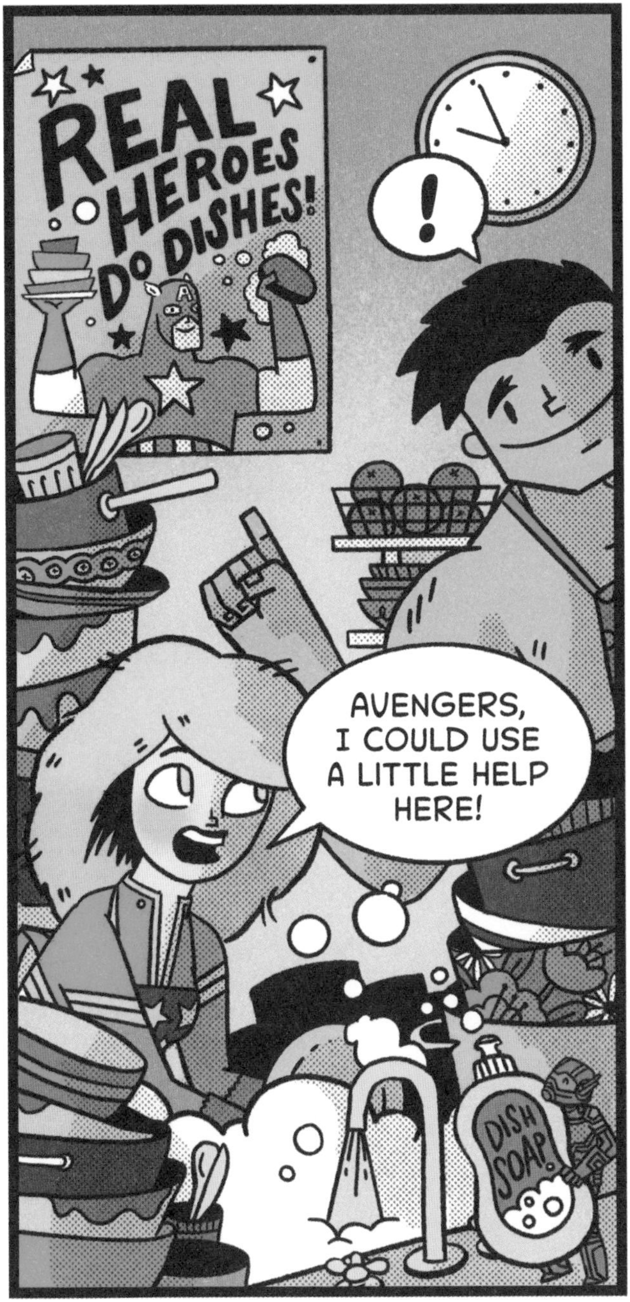
REAL HEROES DO DISHES!
!
AVENGERS, I COULD USE A LITTLE HELP HERE!
DISH SOAP

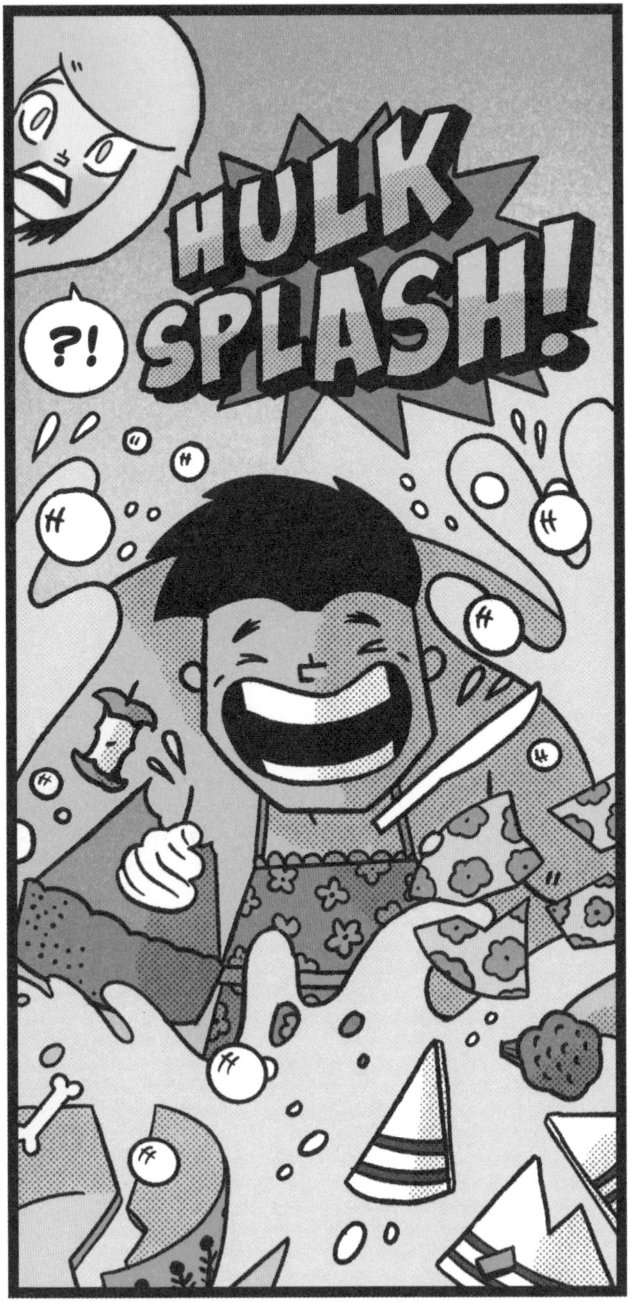
HULK SPLASH!
?!

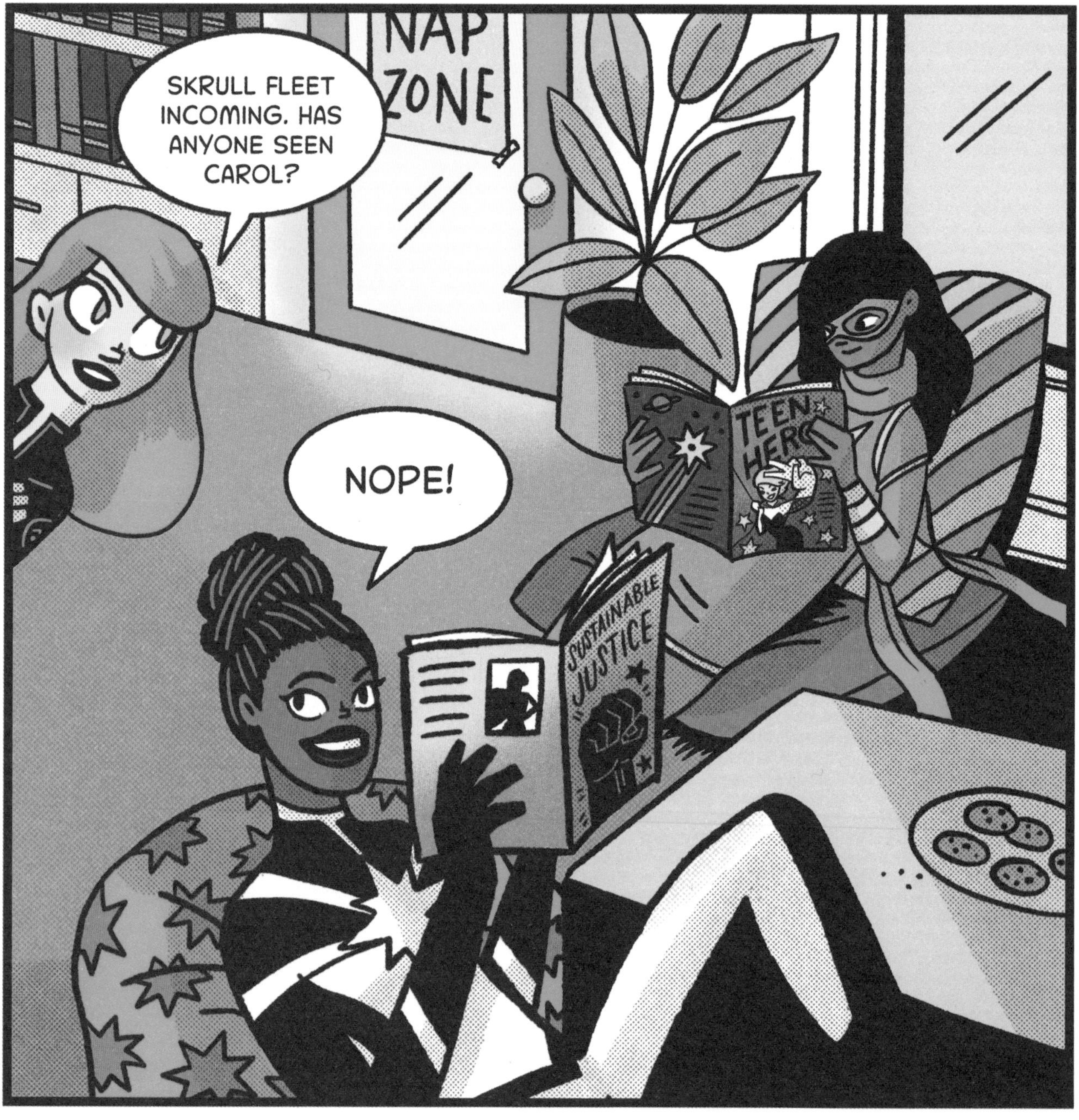
NAP ZONE
SKRULL FLEET INCOMING. HAS ANYONE SEEN CAROL?
NOPE!
TEEN HERO
SUSTAINABLE JUSTICE

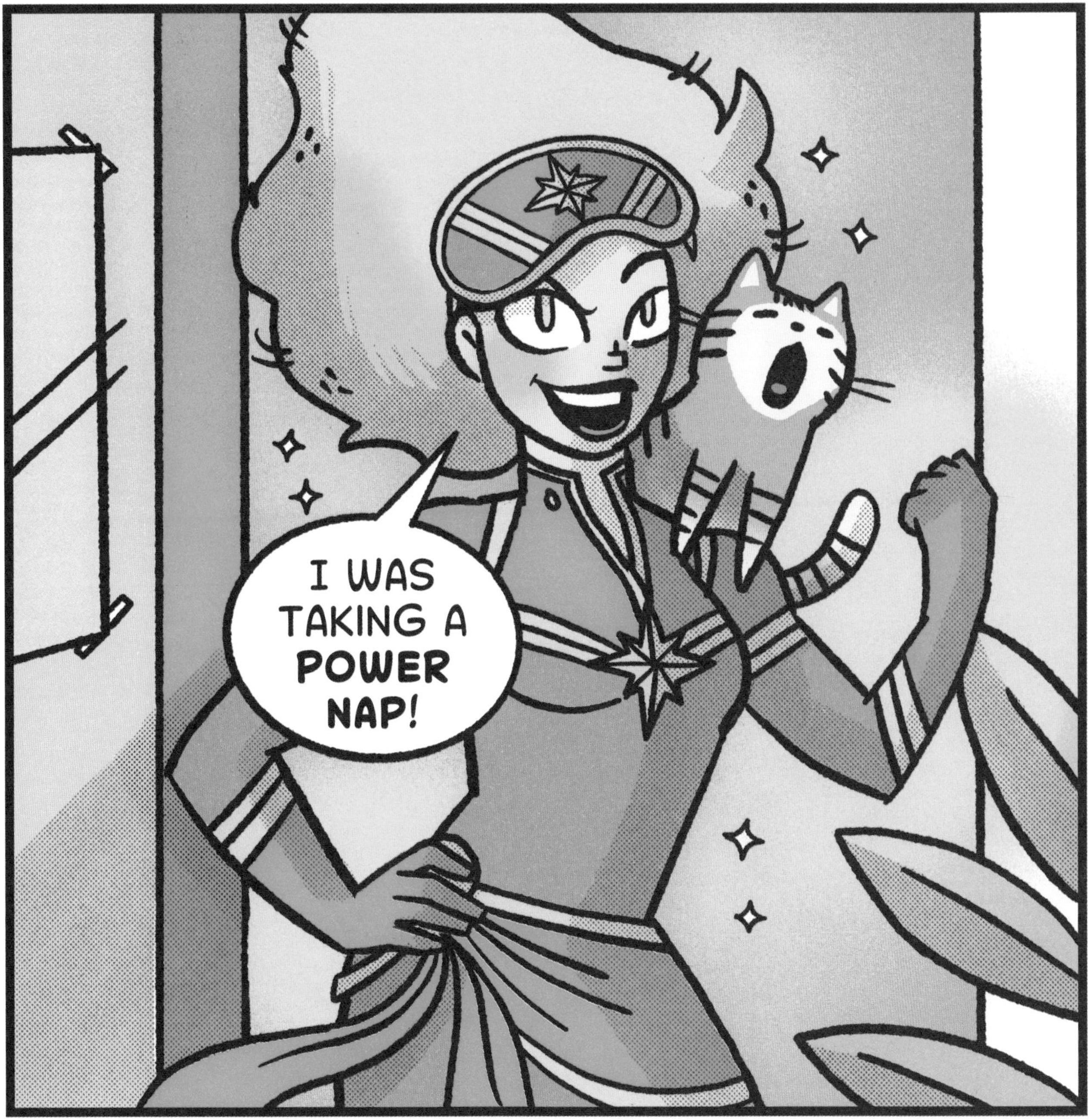
I WAS TAKING A **POWER NAP!**

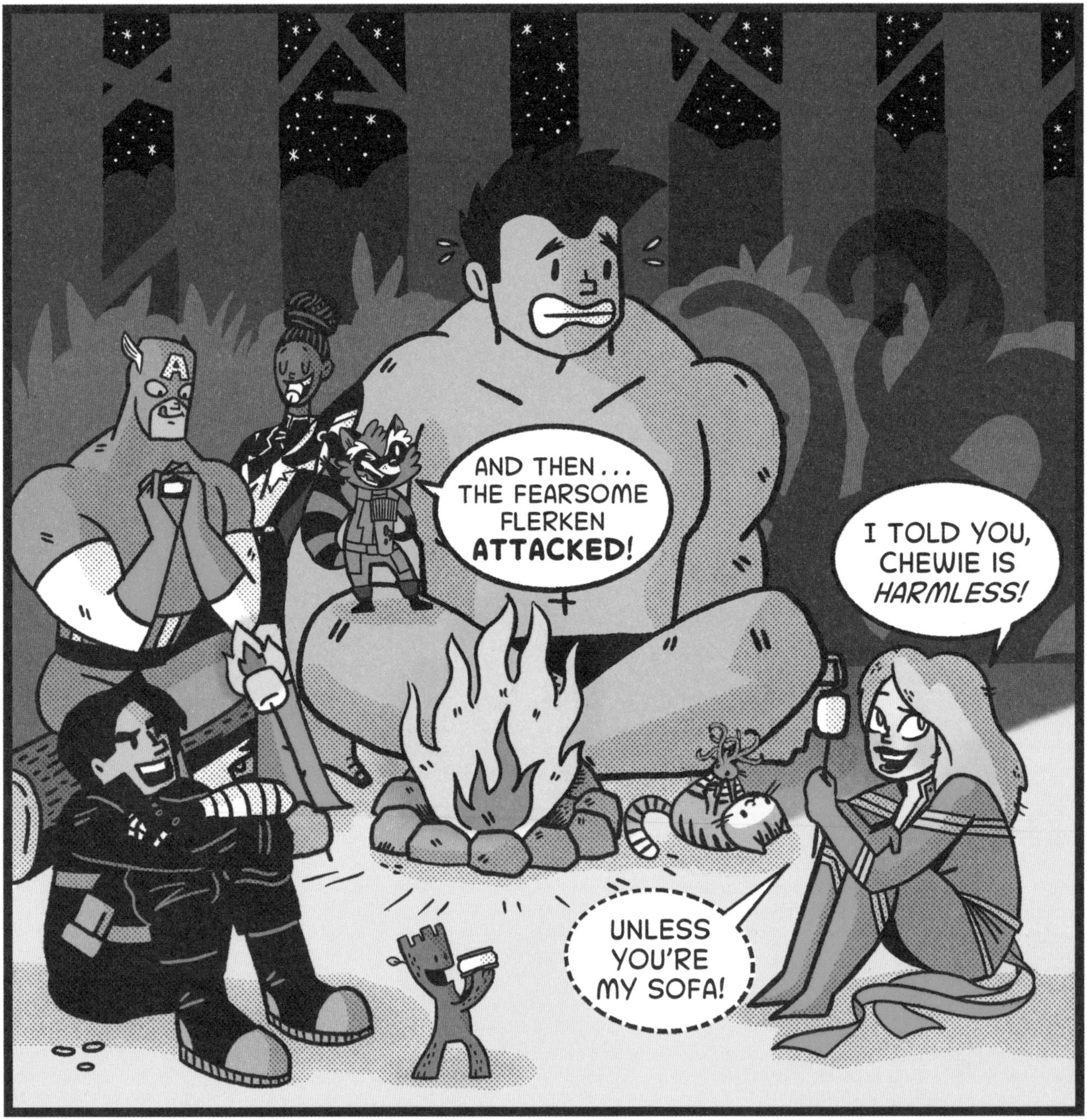
AND THEN . . . THE FEARSOME FLERKEN **ATTACKED!**
I TOLD YOU, CHEWIE IS *HARMLESS!*
UNLESS YOU'RE MY SOFA!

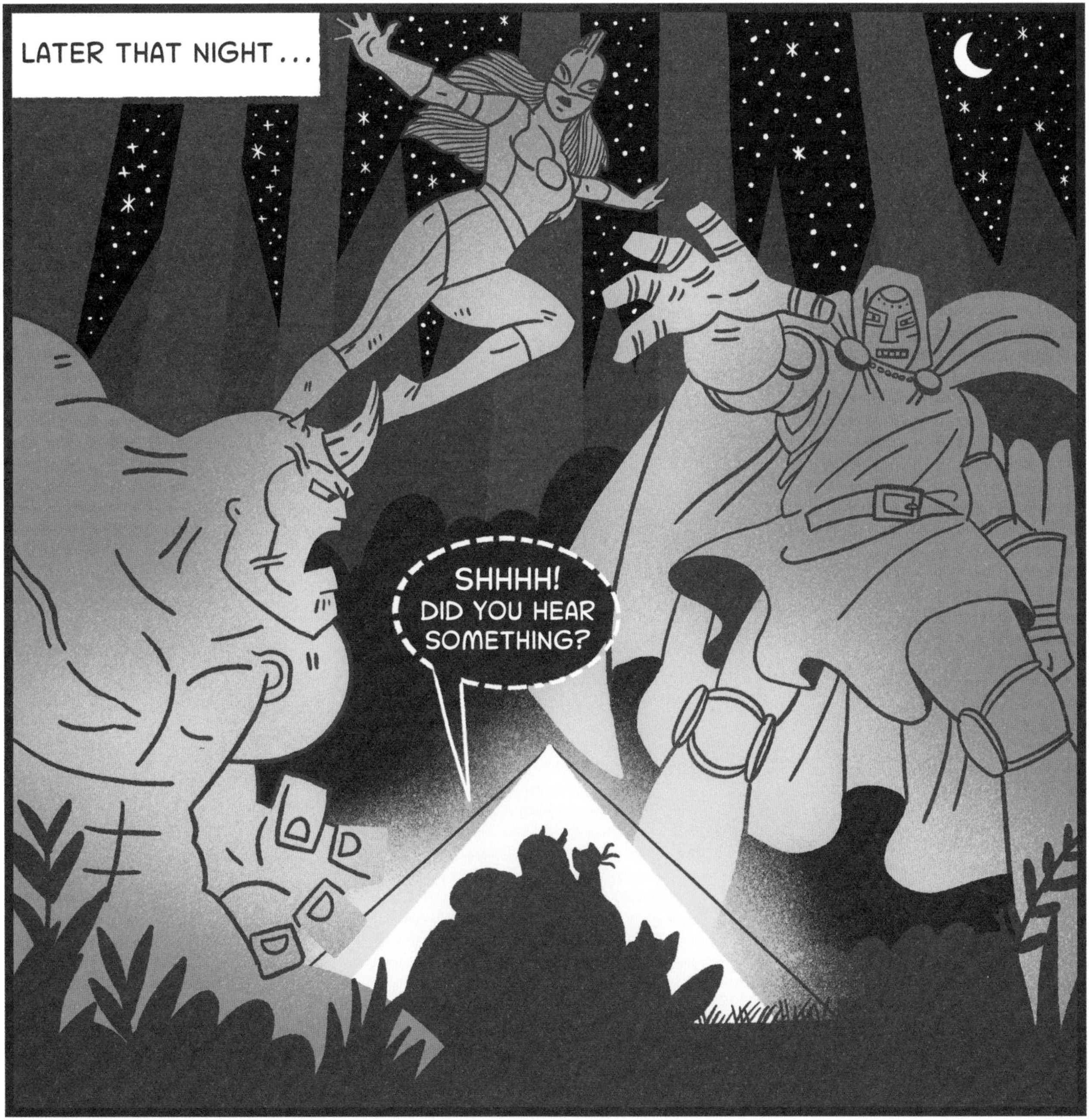
LATER THAT NIGHT . . .
SHHHH! DID YOU HEAR SOMETHING?

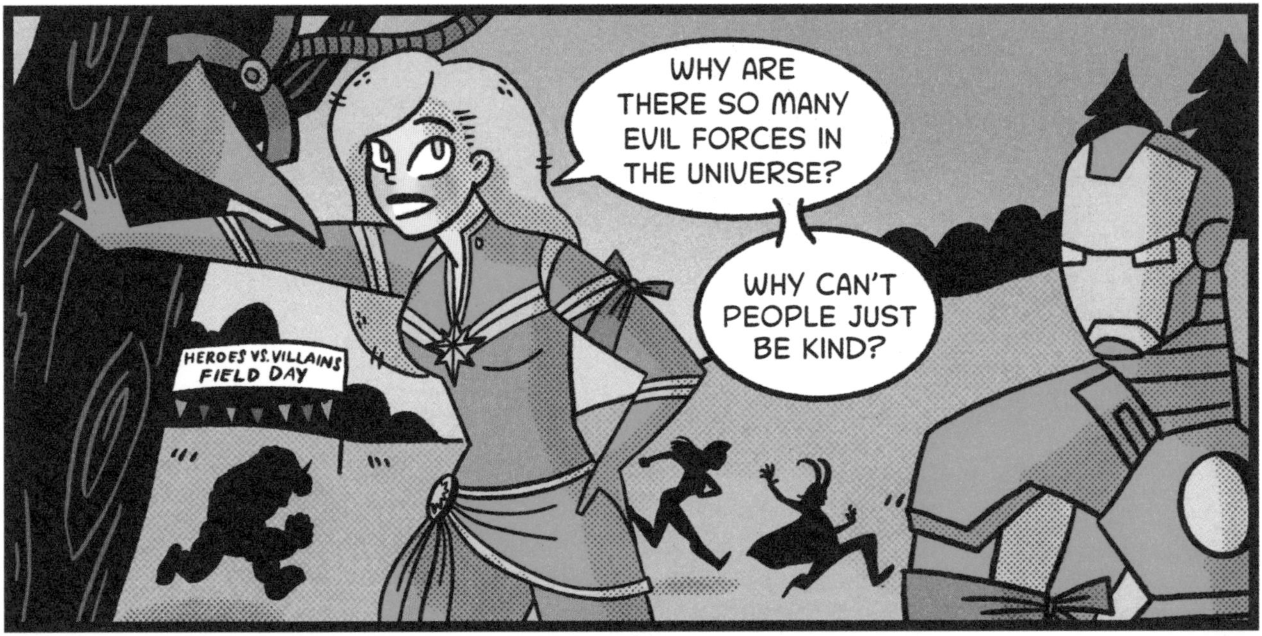
WHY ARE THERE SO MANY EVIL FORCES IN THE UNIVERSE?
WHY CAN'T PEOPLE JUST BE KIND?
HEROES VS. VILLAINS FIELD DAY

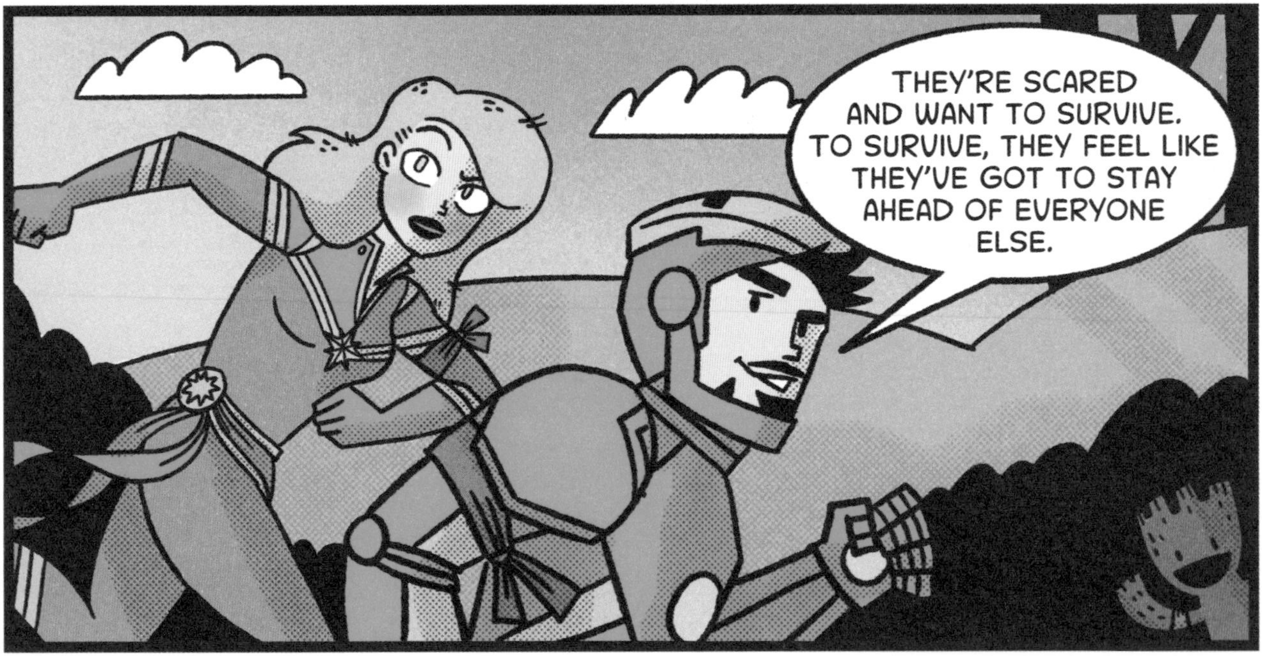
THEY'RE SCARED AND WANT TO SURVIVE. TO SURVIVE, THEY FEEL LIKE THEY'VE GOT TO STAY AHEAD OF EVERYONE ELSE.

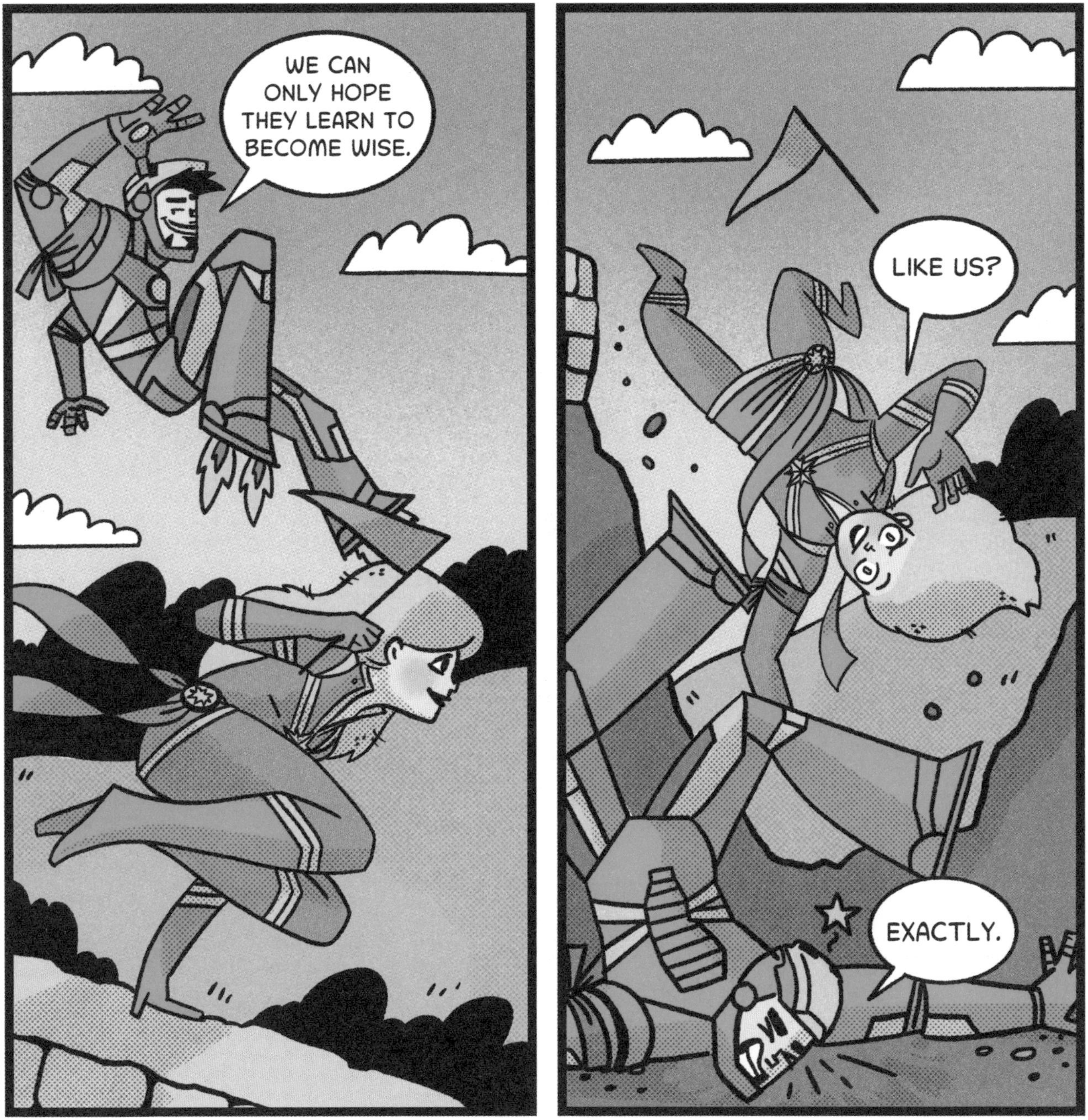
WE CAN ONLY HOPE THEY LEARN TO BECOME WISE.
LIKE US?
EXACTLY.

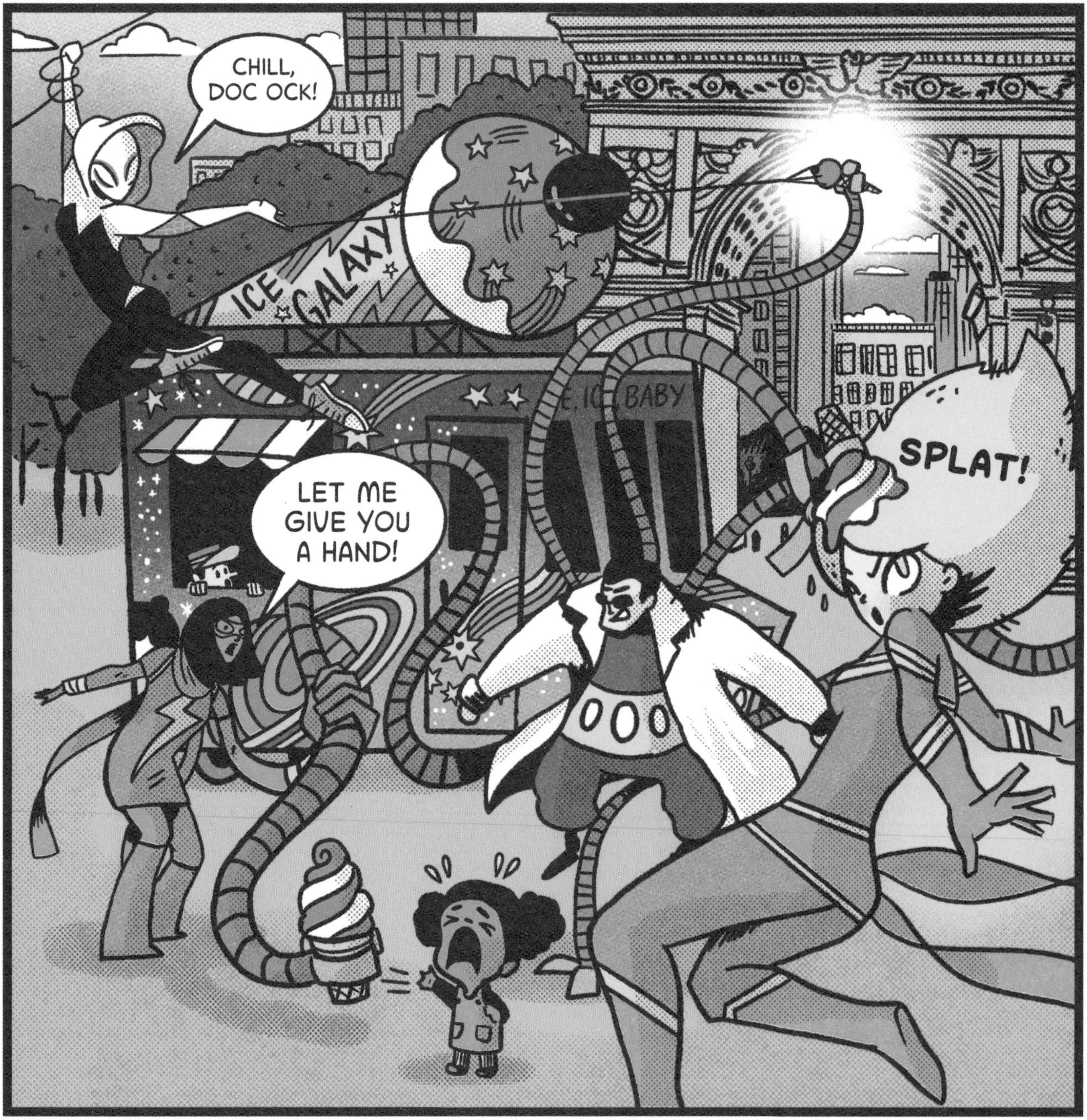
CHILL, DOC OCK!
ICE GALAXY
ICE, ICE, BABY
LET ME GIVE YOU A HAND!
SPLAT!

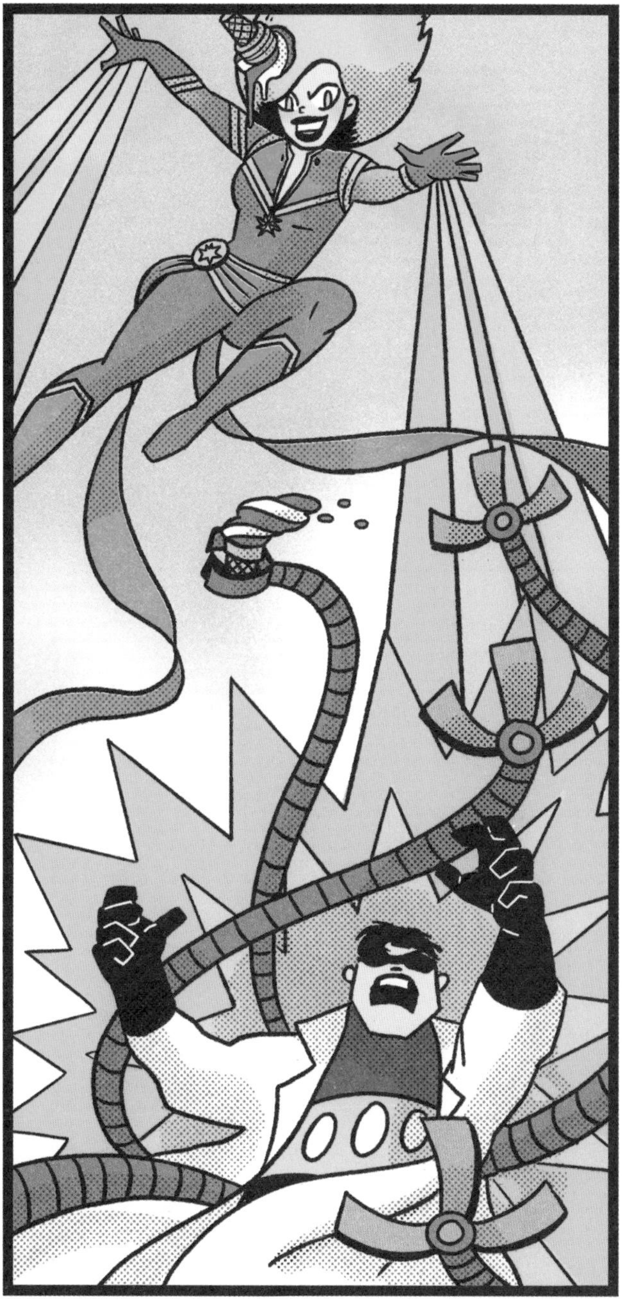

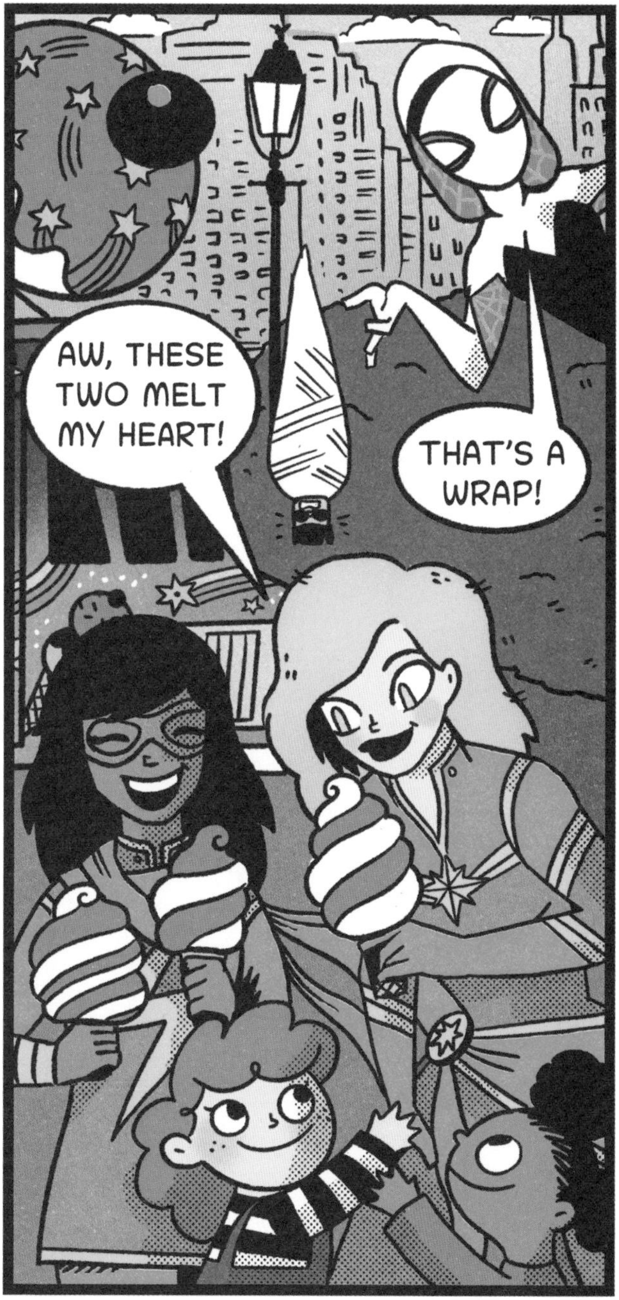
AW, THESE TWO MELT MY HEART!
THAT'S A WRAP!

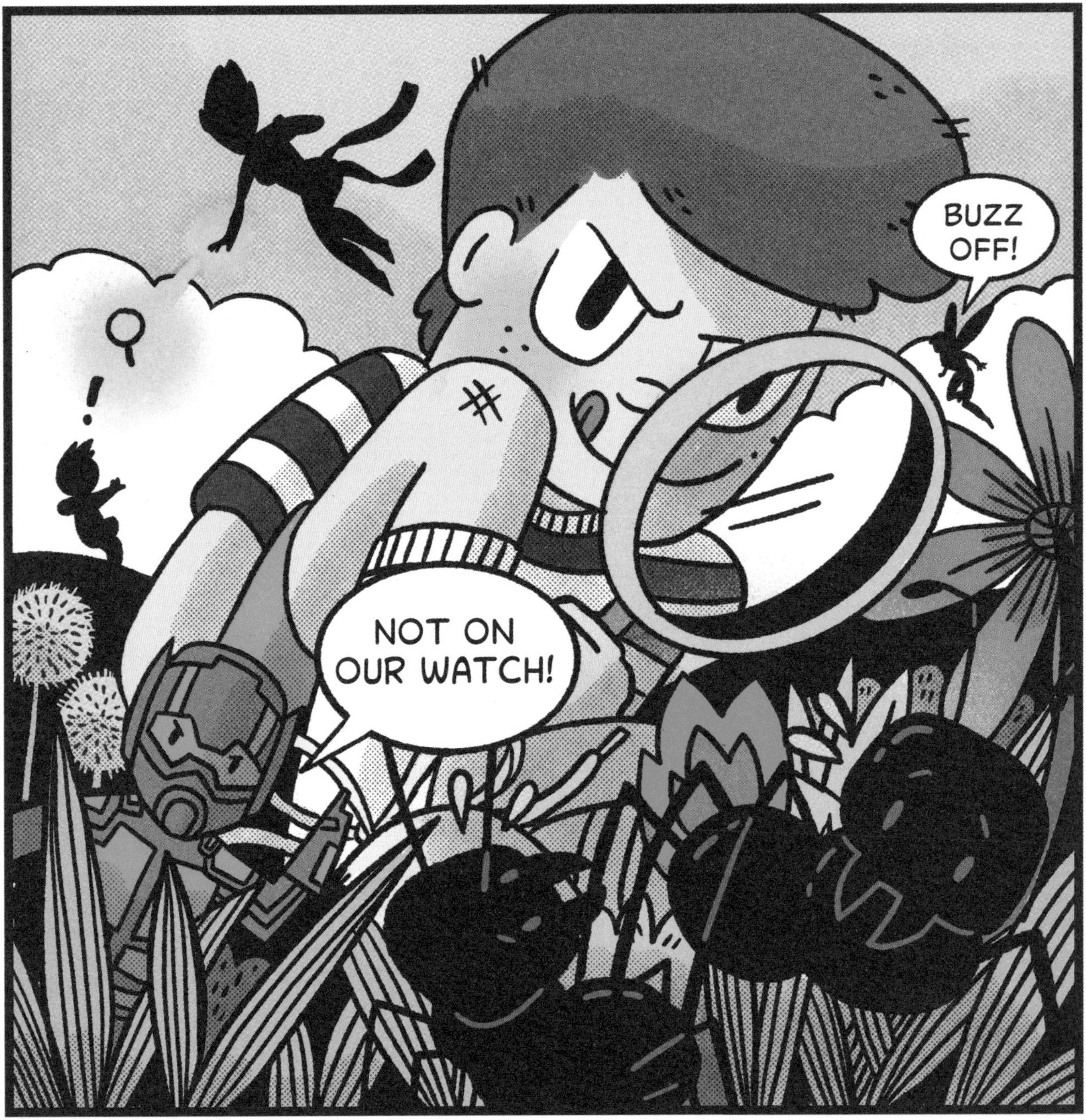
BUZZ OFF!
NOT ON OUR WATCH!

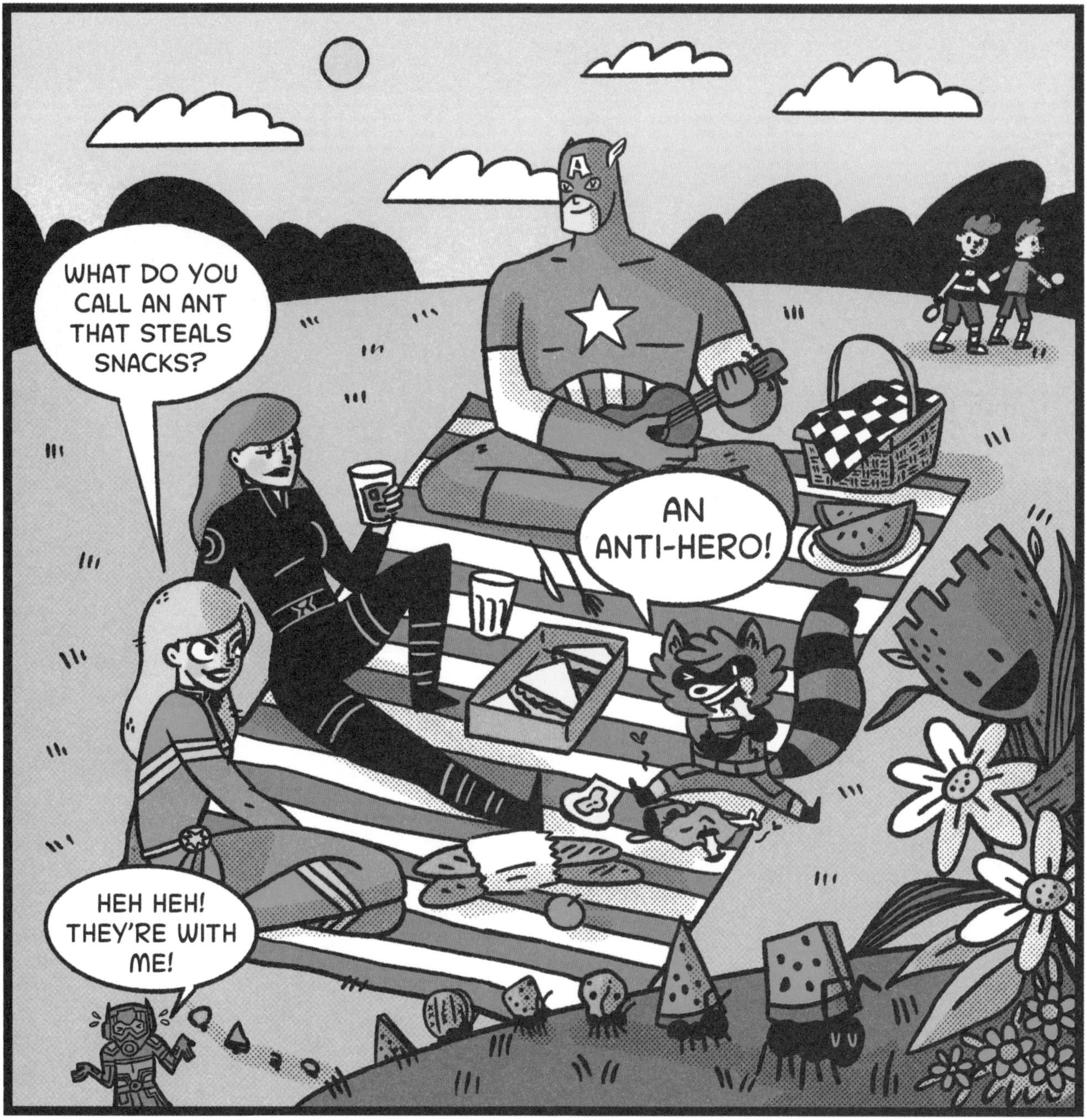
WHAT DO YOU CALL AN ANT THAT STEALS SNACKS?
AN ANTI-HERO!
HEH HEH! THEY'RE WITH ME!

YOU'VE REACHED MY VOICEMAIL. I'M ON VACATION, HAVING A BLAST! IF THIS IS AN EMERGENCY, PLEASE CALL NICK FURY...
HUH?

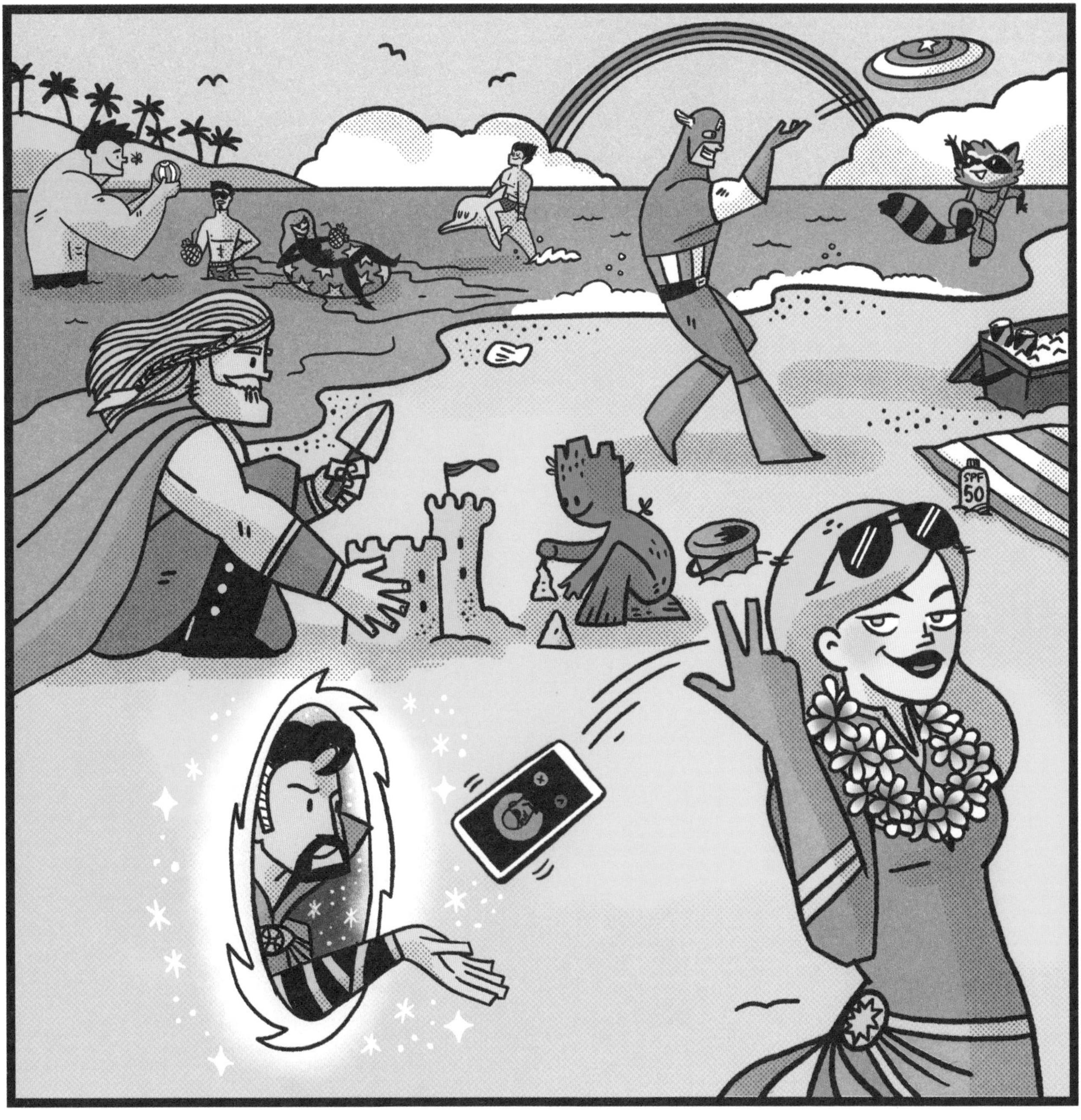
SPF
50

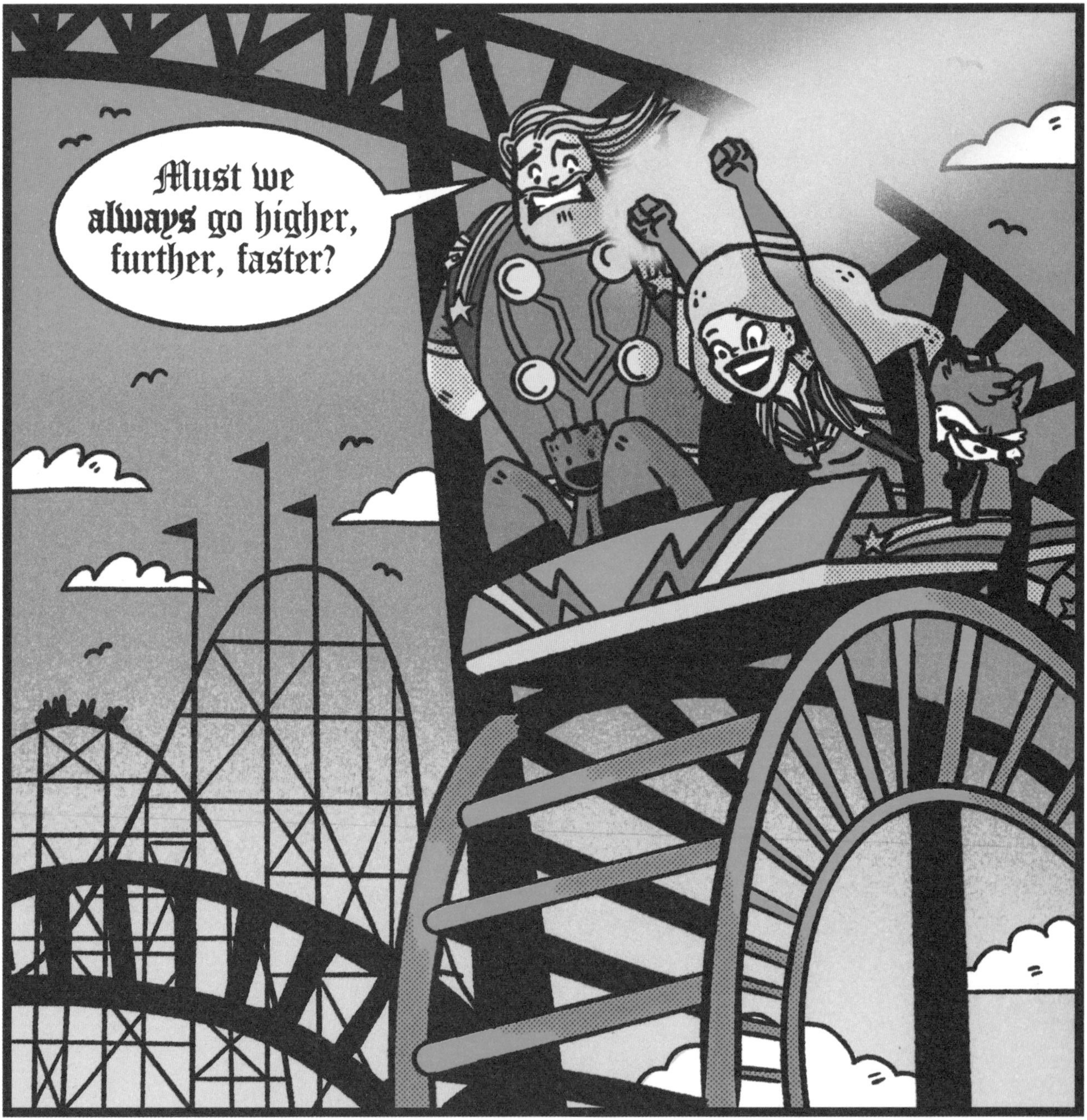
Must we **always** go higher, further, faster?

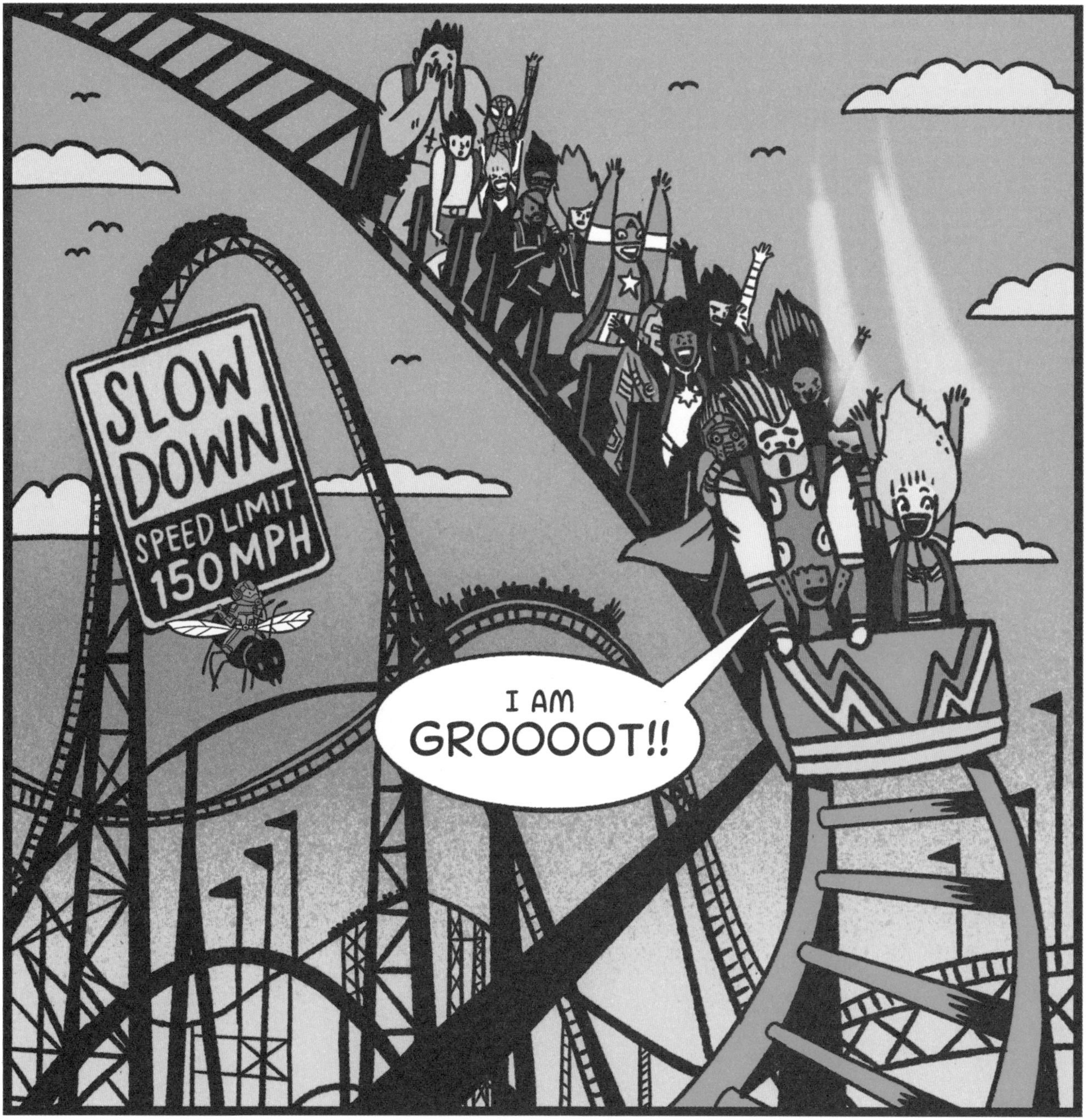
SLOW DOWN
SPEED LIMIT 150 MPH
I AM GROOOOT!!

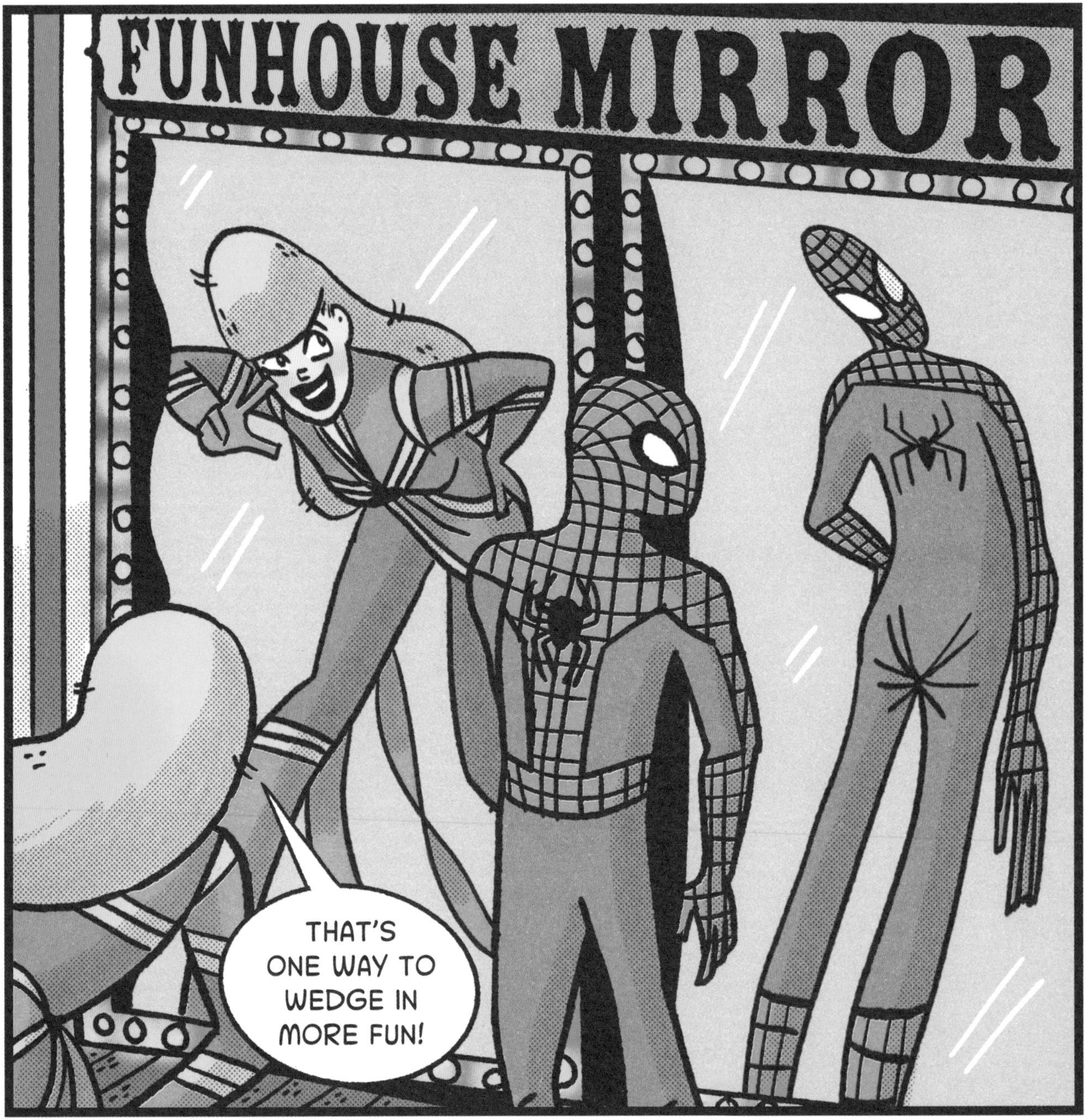
FUNHOUSE MIRROR
THAT'S ONE WAY TO WEDGE IN MORE FUN!

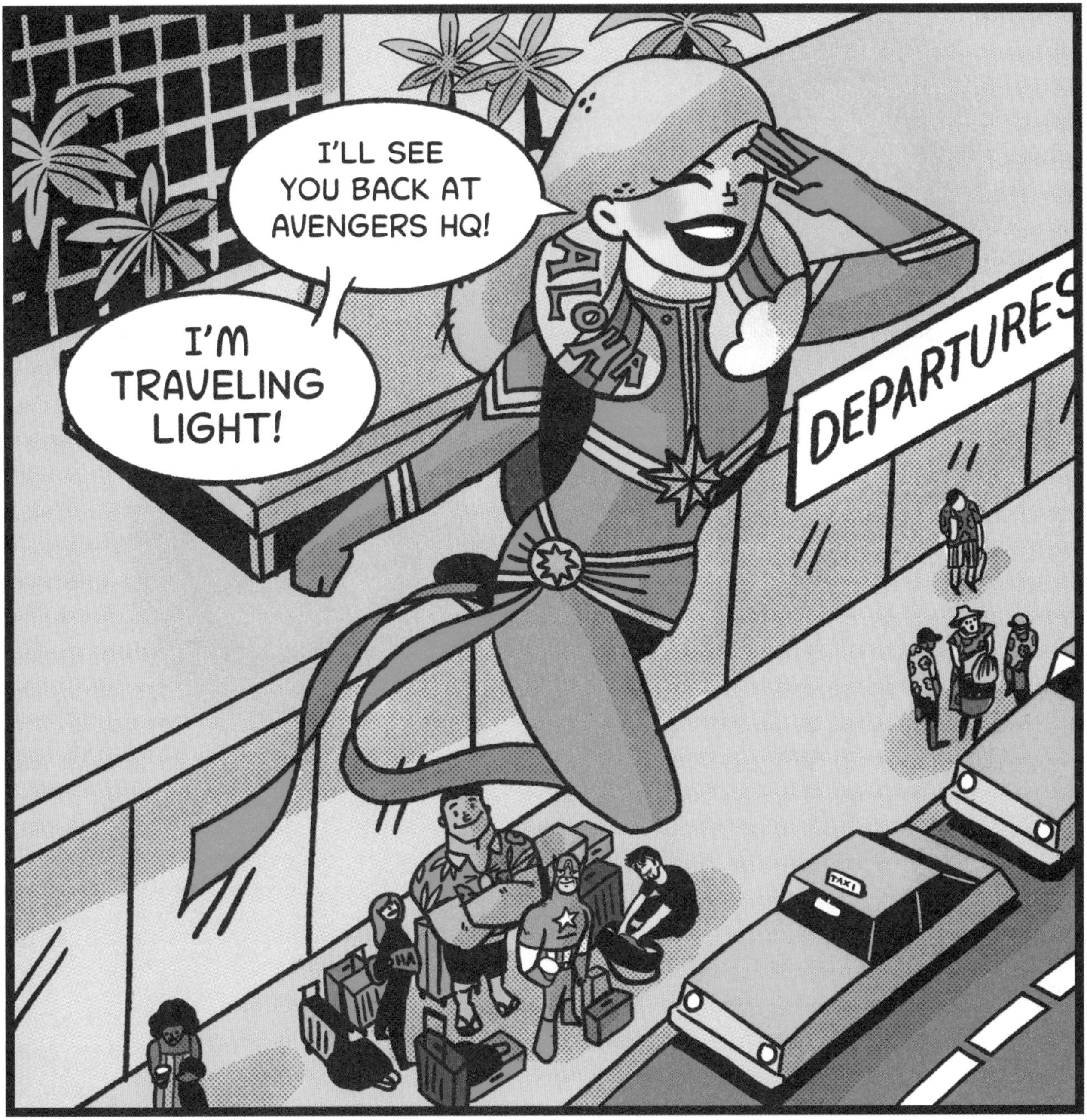
I'LL SEE YOU BACK AT AVENGERS HQ!
I'M TRAVELING LIGHT!
DEPARTURES
ALOHA
TAXI

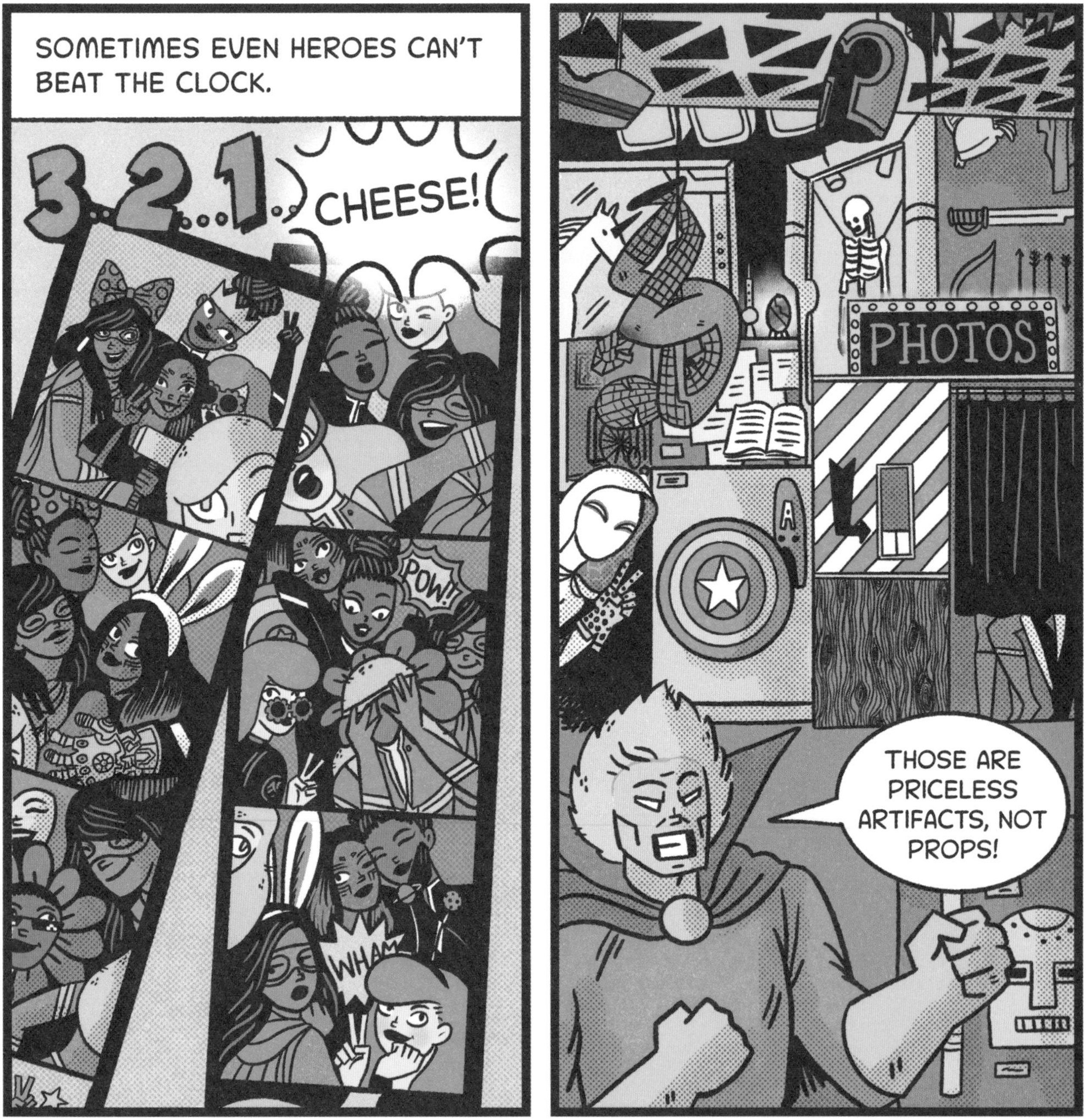
SOMETIMES EVEN HEROES CAN'T BEAT THE CLOCK.
3..2..1..
CHEESE!
POW!
WHAM
PHOTOS
THOSE ARE PRICELESS ARTIFACTS, NOT PROPS!

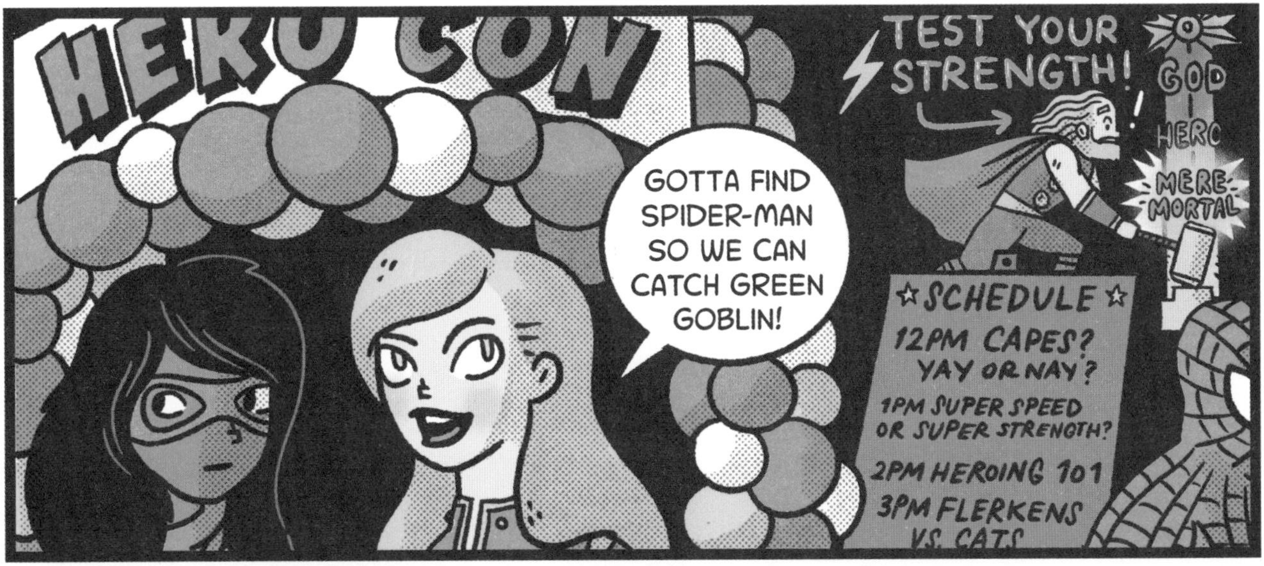
HERO CON
TEST YOUR STRENGTH!
GOD
HERO
MERE MORTAL
GOTTA FIND SPIDER-MAN SO WE CAN CATCH GREEN GOBLIN!
☆SCHEDULE☆
12PM CAPES? YAY OR NAY?
1PM SUPER SPEED OR SUPER STRENGTH?
2PM HEROING 101
3PM FLERKENS VS. CATS

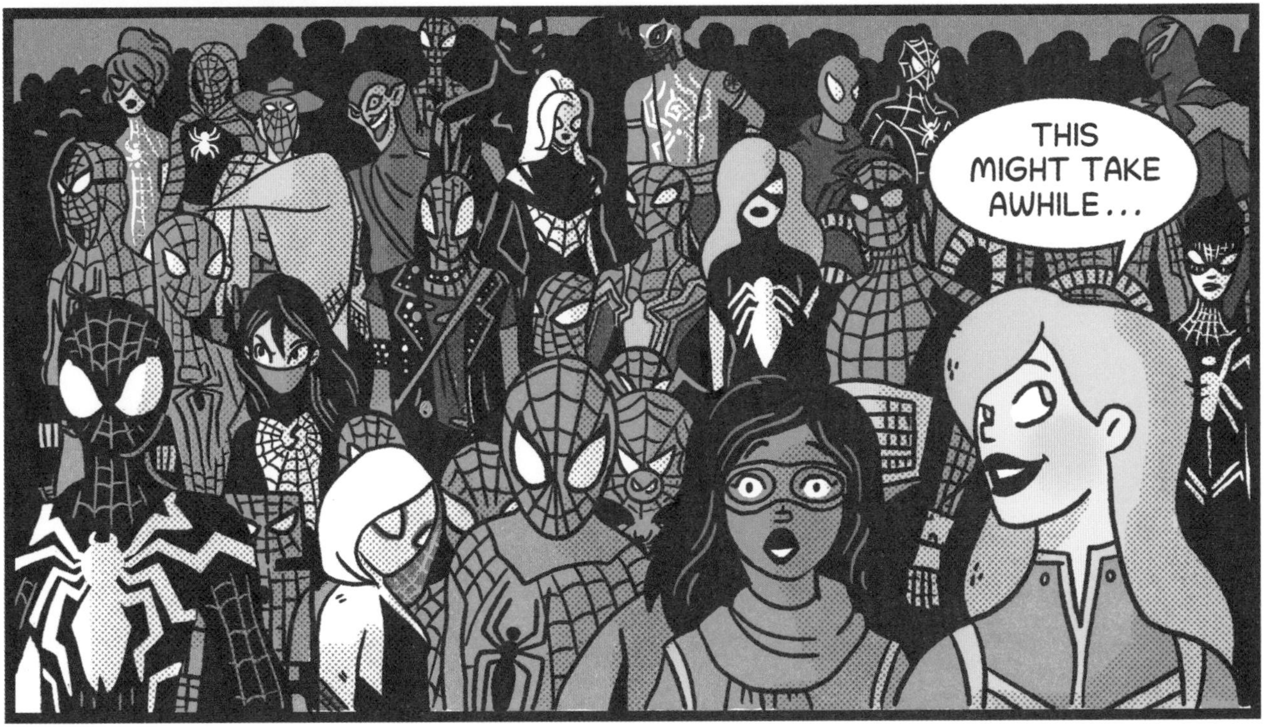
THIS MIGHT TAKE AWHILE...

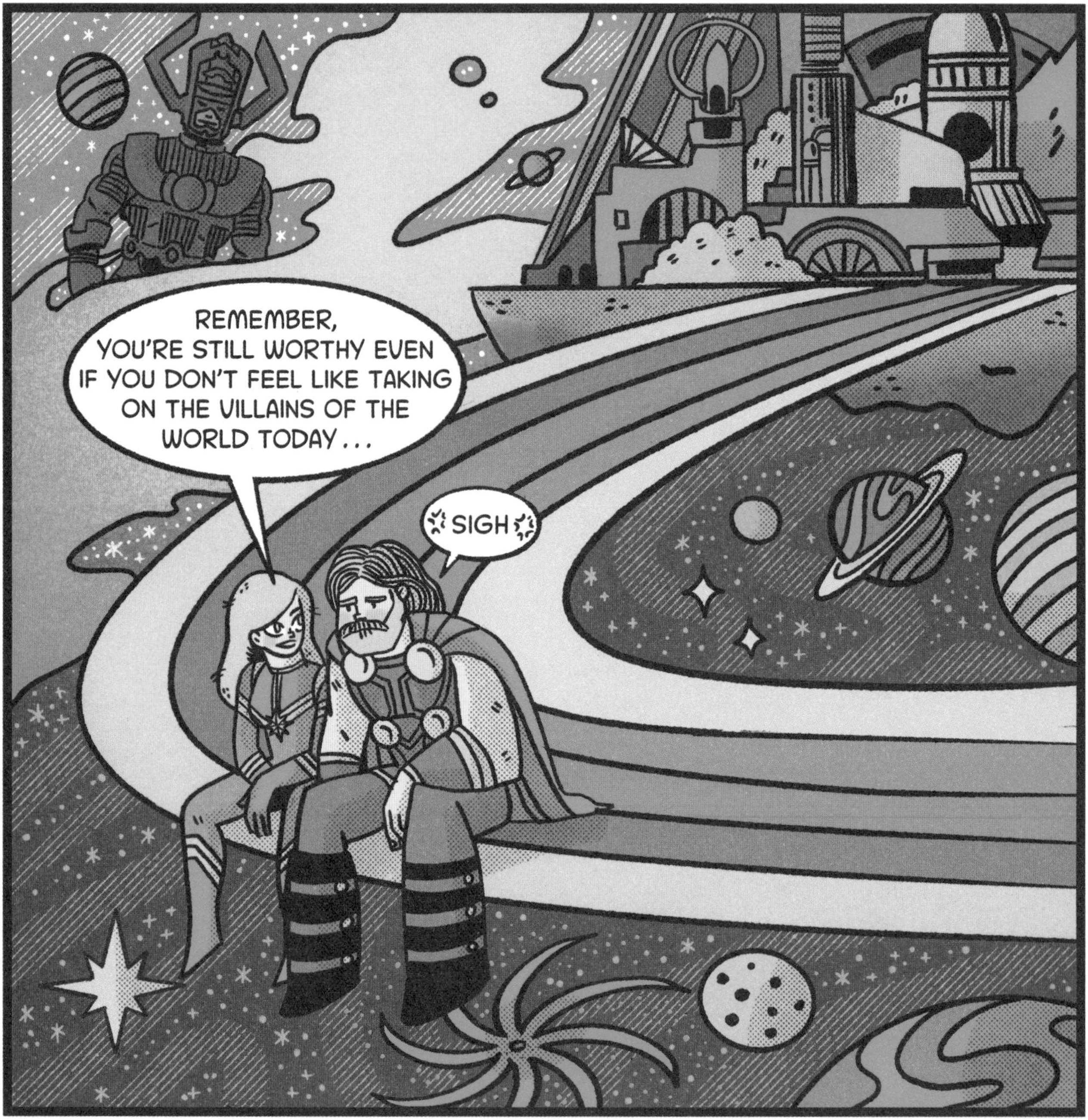
REMEMBER, YOU'RE STILL WORTHY EVEN IF YOU DON'T FEEL LIKE TAKING ON THE VILLAINS OF THE WORLD TODAY...
SIGH

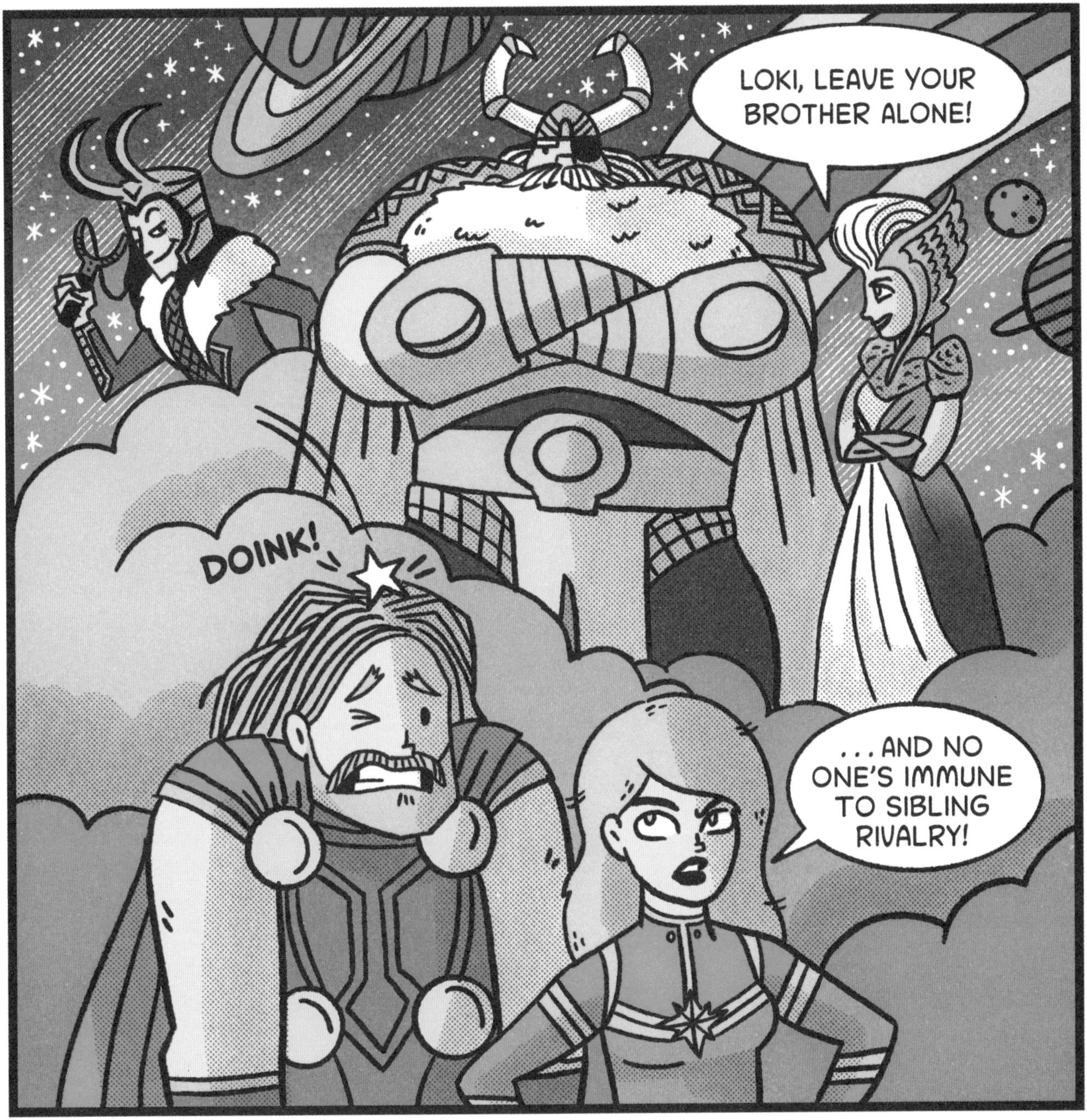
LOKI, LEAVE YOUR BROTHER ALONE!
DOINK!
. . . AND NO ONE'S IMMUNE TO SIBLING RIVALRY!

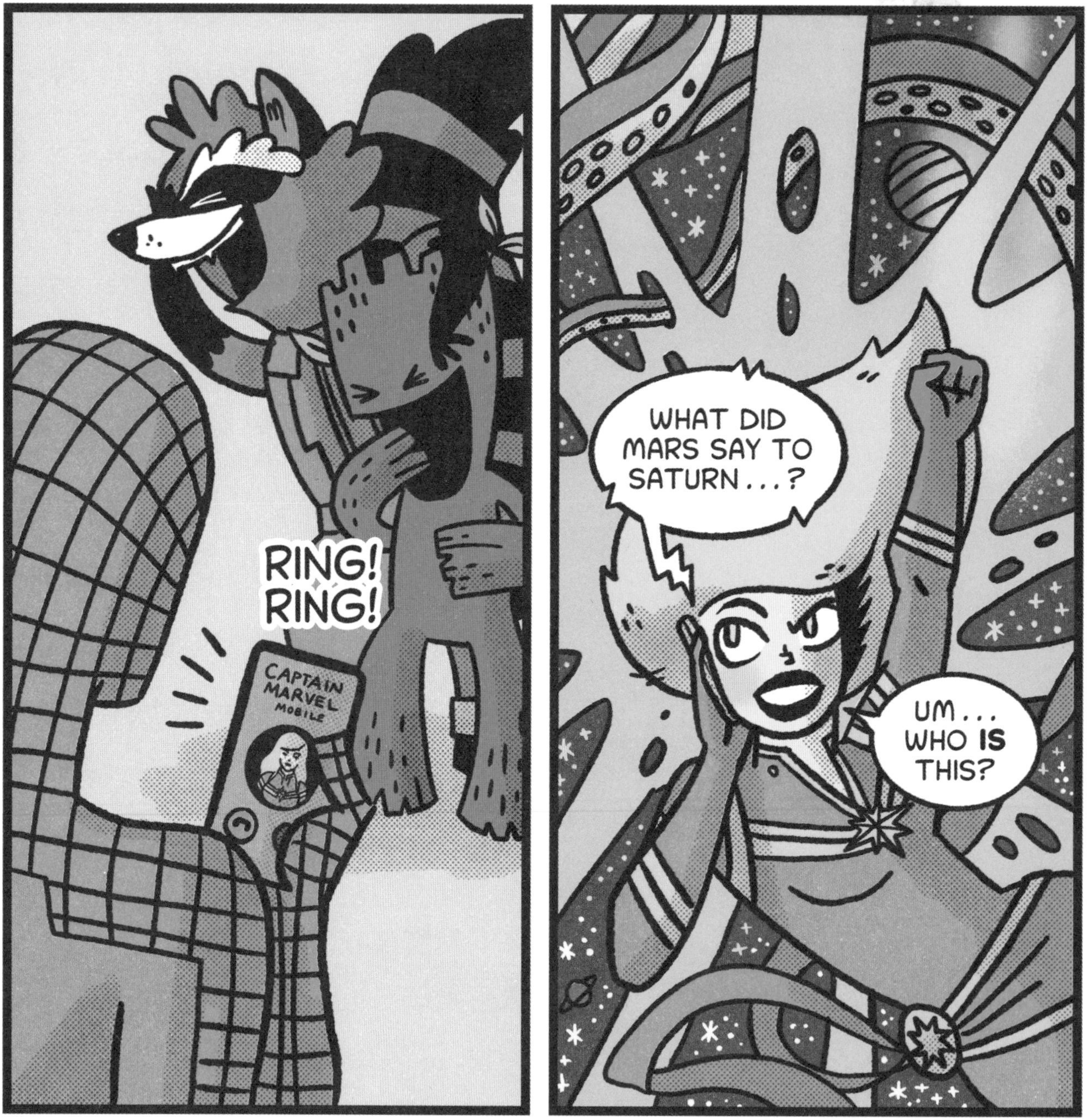
RING! RING!
CAPTAIN MARVEL MOBILE
WHAT DID MARS SAY TO SATURN...?
UM... WHO **IS** THIS?

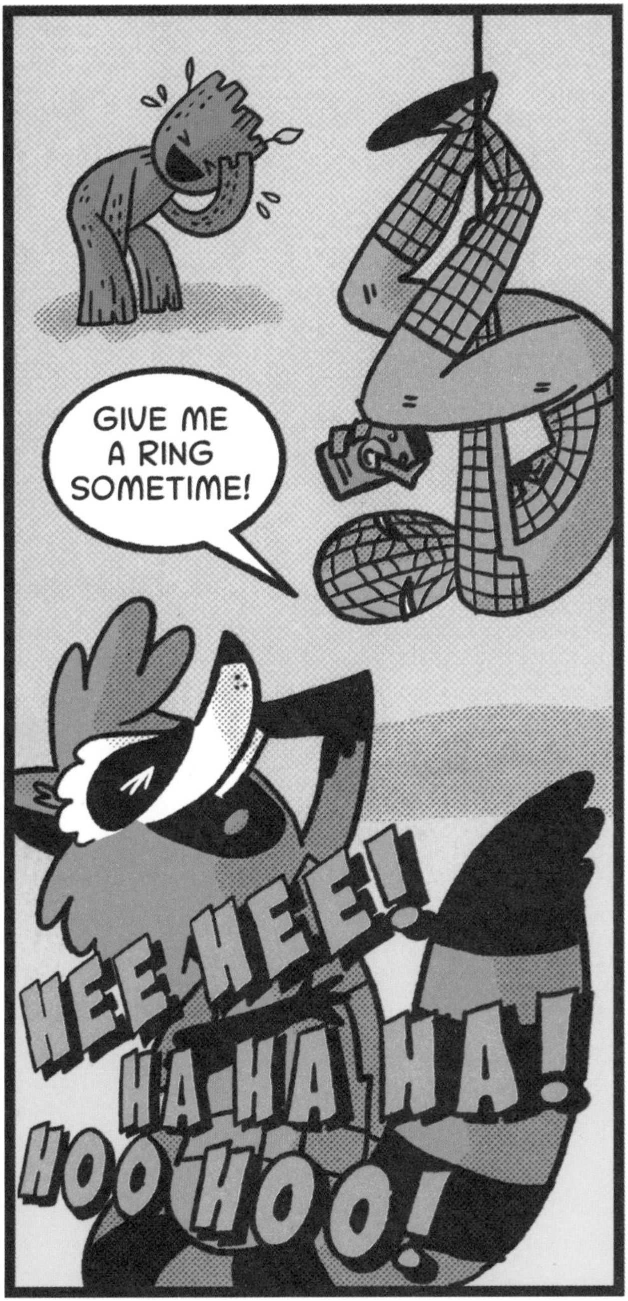
GIVE ME A RING SOMETIME!
HEE-HEE!
HA-HA-HA-HA!
HOO-HOO!

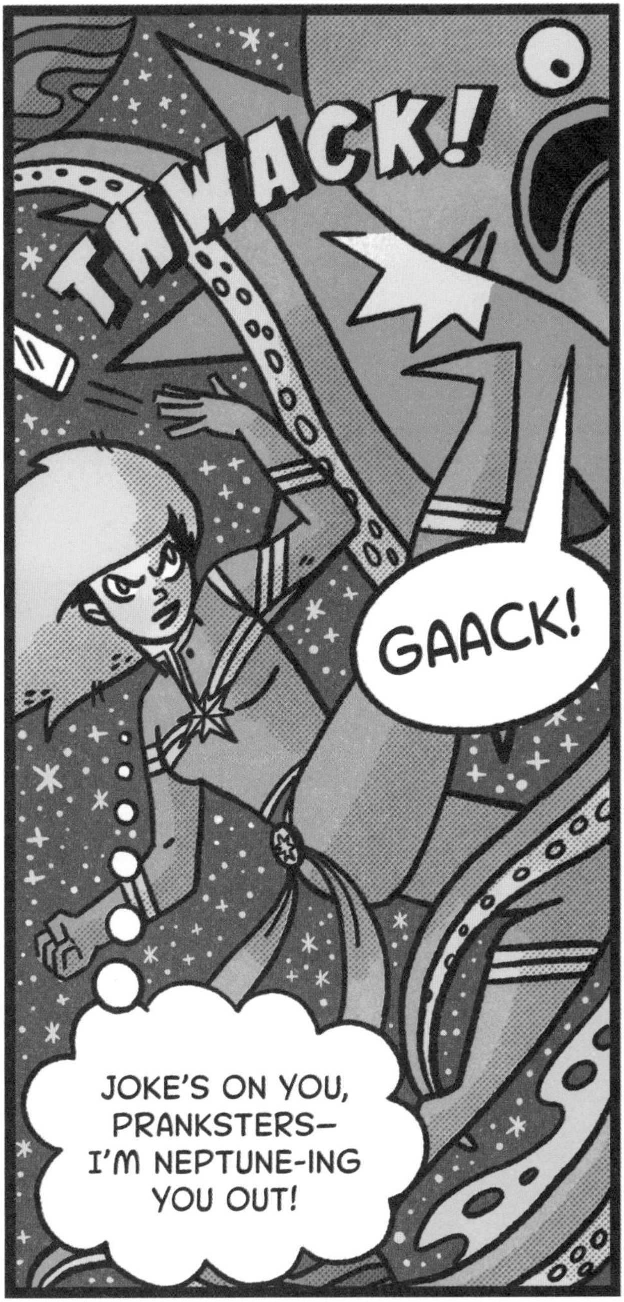
THWACK!
GAACK!
JOKE'S ON YOU, PRANKSTERS— I'M NEPTUNE-ING YOU OUT!

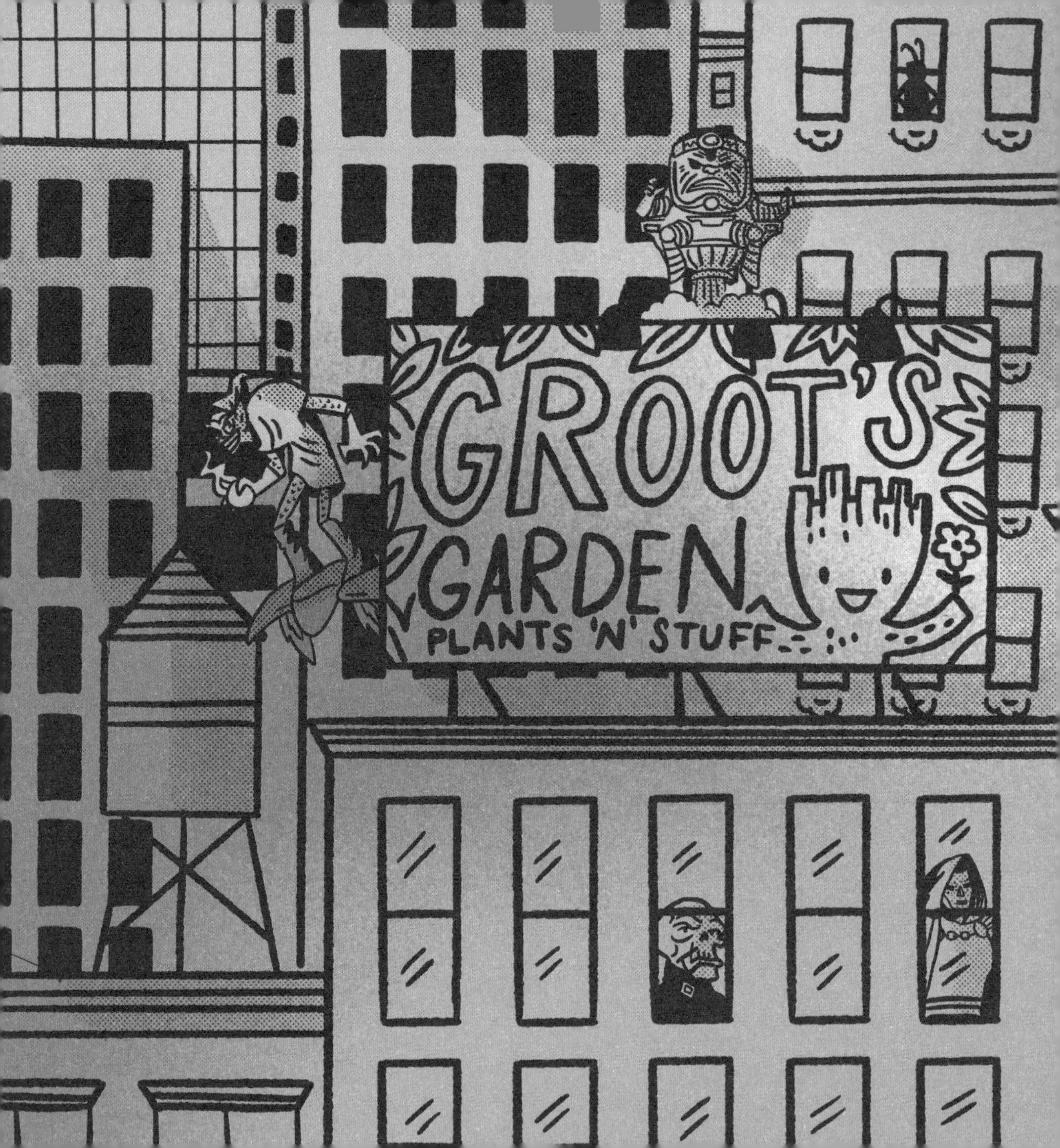
GROOT'S
GARDEN
PLANTS 'N' STUFF

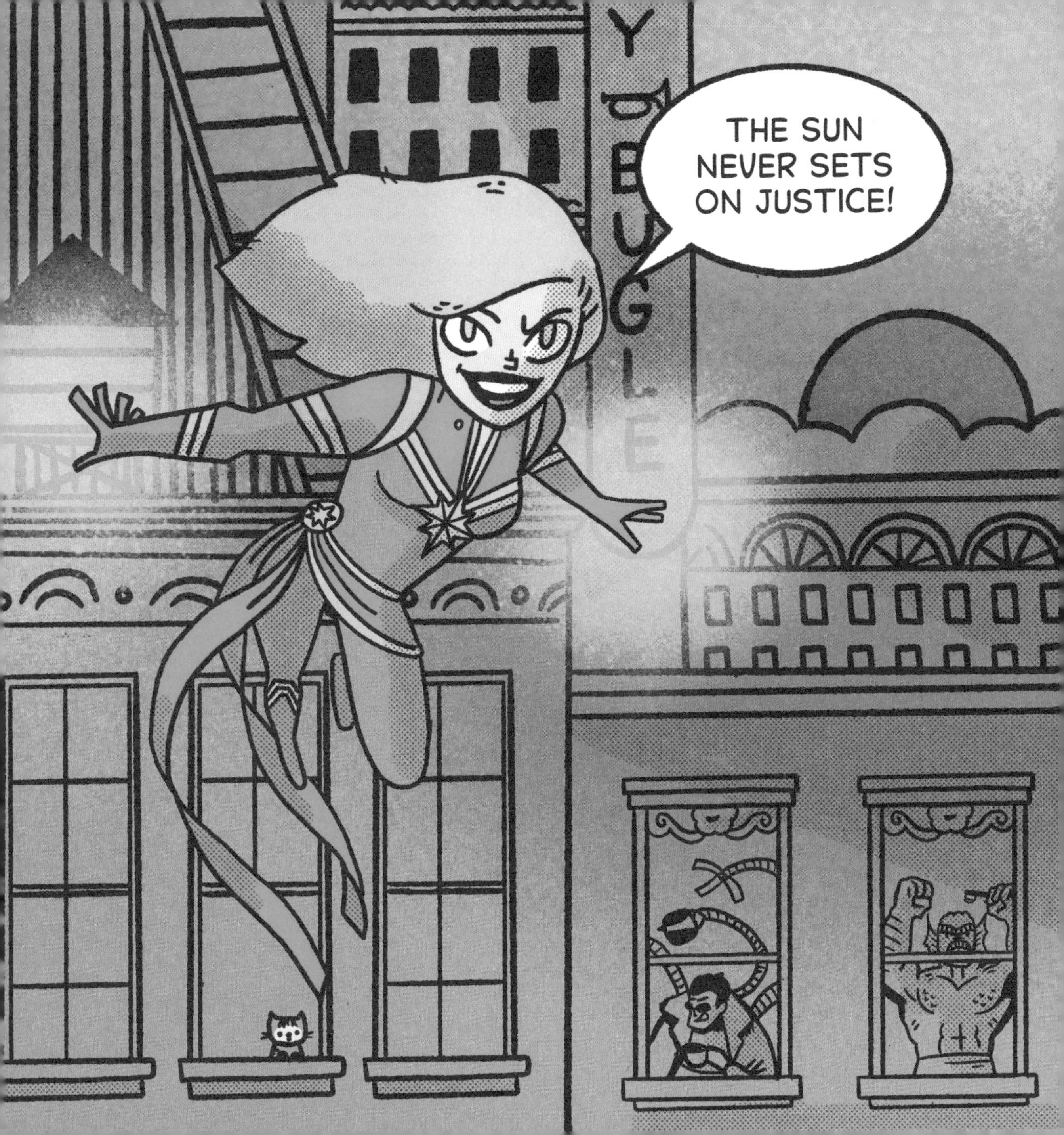
THE SUN NEVER SETS ON JUSTICE!

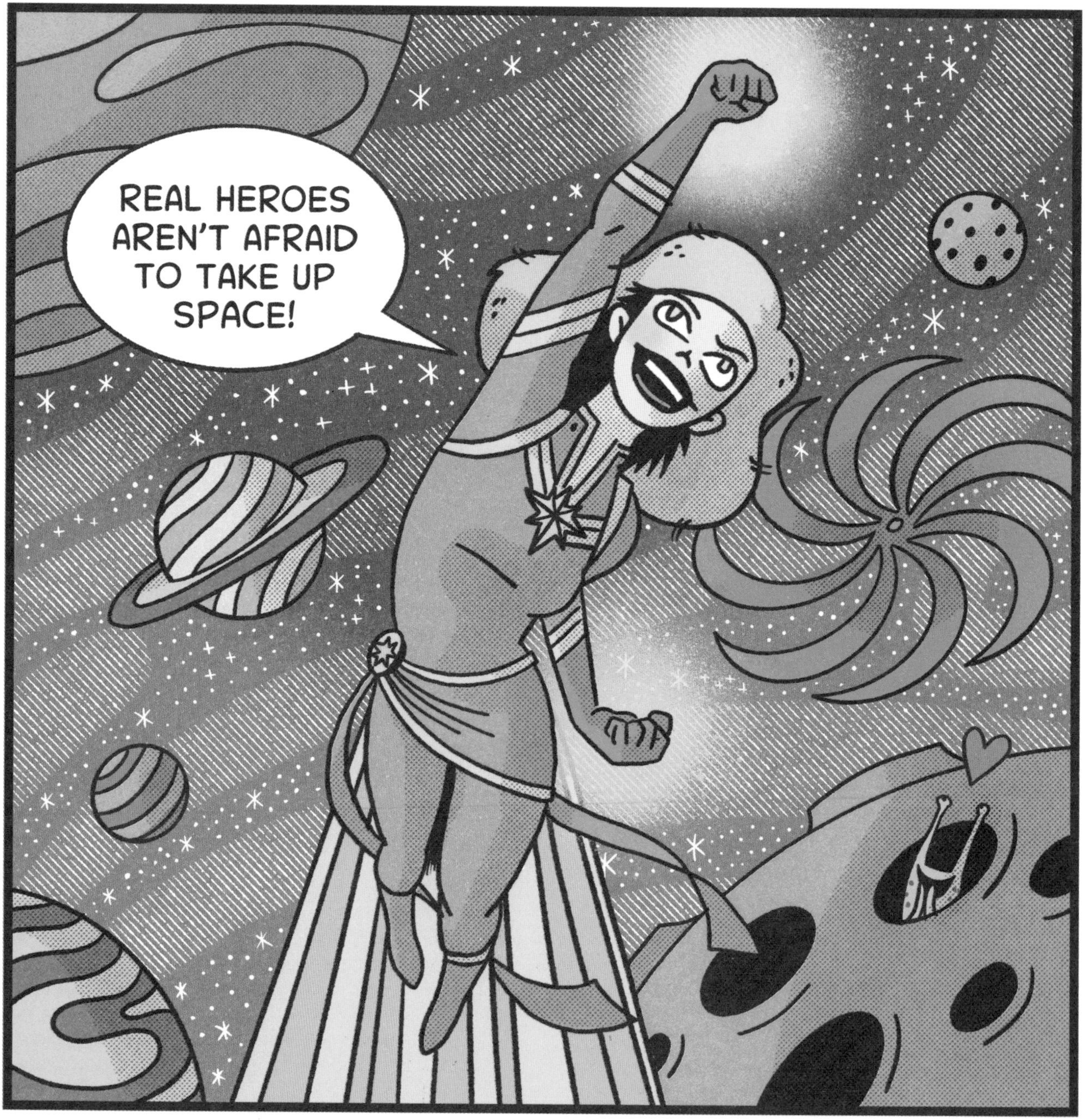
REAL HEROES AREN'T AFRAID TO TAKE UP SPACE!

ABOUT THE CREATORS

THE MOYLE SISTERS ARE THE BESTSELLING CREATIVE TEAM BEHIND OVER 20 ILLUSTRATED BOOKS FOR ALL AGES INCLUDING *MY MOM IS MAGICAL!*, *GO GET 'EM, TIGER!*, AND THE GRAPHIC NOVEL SERIES THE COSMIC ADVENTURES OF ASTRID AND STELLA. WHEN NOT SAVING PLANETS, FEEDING THEIR FLERKEN-EQUIVALENTS, AND BATTLING DEMONS (INNER AND OUTER), THEY SPEND THEIR TIME MAKING BOOKS, CARDS, AND GAMES THROUGH THEIR DESIGN STUDIO, HELLO!LUCKY. THAT IS, UNTIL THE NEXT PLANET NEEDS SAVING—WITH A LITTLE LOVE AND FRIENDSHIP, OF COURSE, AND A WHOLE LOT OF PUNS!

WWW.HELLOLUCKY.COM

ACKNOWLEDGMENTS

THANKS TO ERUM KHAN, ANNE HELTZEL, LAUREN BISOM, CAITLIN O'CONNELL, AMY ACHAIBOU, KELLY BRAUN, CHARLOTTE APPLEBAUM, AND BRANN GARVEY—OUR OUT-OF-THIS-WORLD EDITORIAL AND CREATIVE TEAM. THANK YOU TO ANDREW SMITH, JODY MOSLEY, AND MEREDITH MUNDY FOR BRINGING US THE IDEA FOR THIS SERIES, AND FOR GIVING US THE CHANCE TO CREATE CHILDREN'S BOOKS. MOST OF ALL, THANK YOU TO OUR FAMILIES FOR YOUR LOVE AND SUPPORT.

LIBRARY OF CONGRESS CONTROL NUMBER
2023945802

ISBN 978-1-4197-6983-2

© 2024 MARVEL

WRITTEN BY SABRINA MOYLE
ILLUSTRATIONS BY EUNICE MOYLE
DESIGN BY AMY ACHAIBOU

PRINTED AND BOUND IN CHINA
10 9 8 7 6 5 4 3 2 1

ABRAMS BOOKS FOR YOUNG READERS ARE AVAILABLE AT SPECIAL DISCOUNTS WHEN PURCHASED IN QUANTITY FOR PREMIUMS AND PROMOTIONS AS WELL AS FUNDRAISING OR EDUCATIONAL USE. SPECIAL EDITIONS CAN ALSO BE CREATED TO SPECIFICATION. FOR DETAILS, CONTACT SPECIALSALES@ABRAMSBOOKS.COM OR THE ADDRESS BELOW.

ABRAMS The Art of Books
195 Broadway, New York, NY 10007
abramsbooks.com

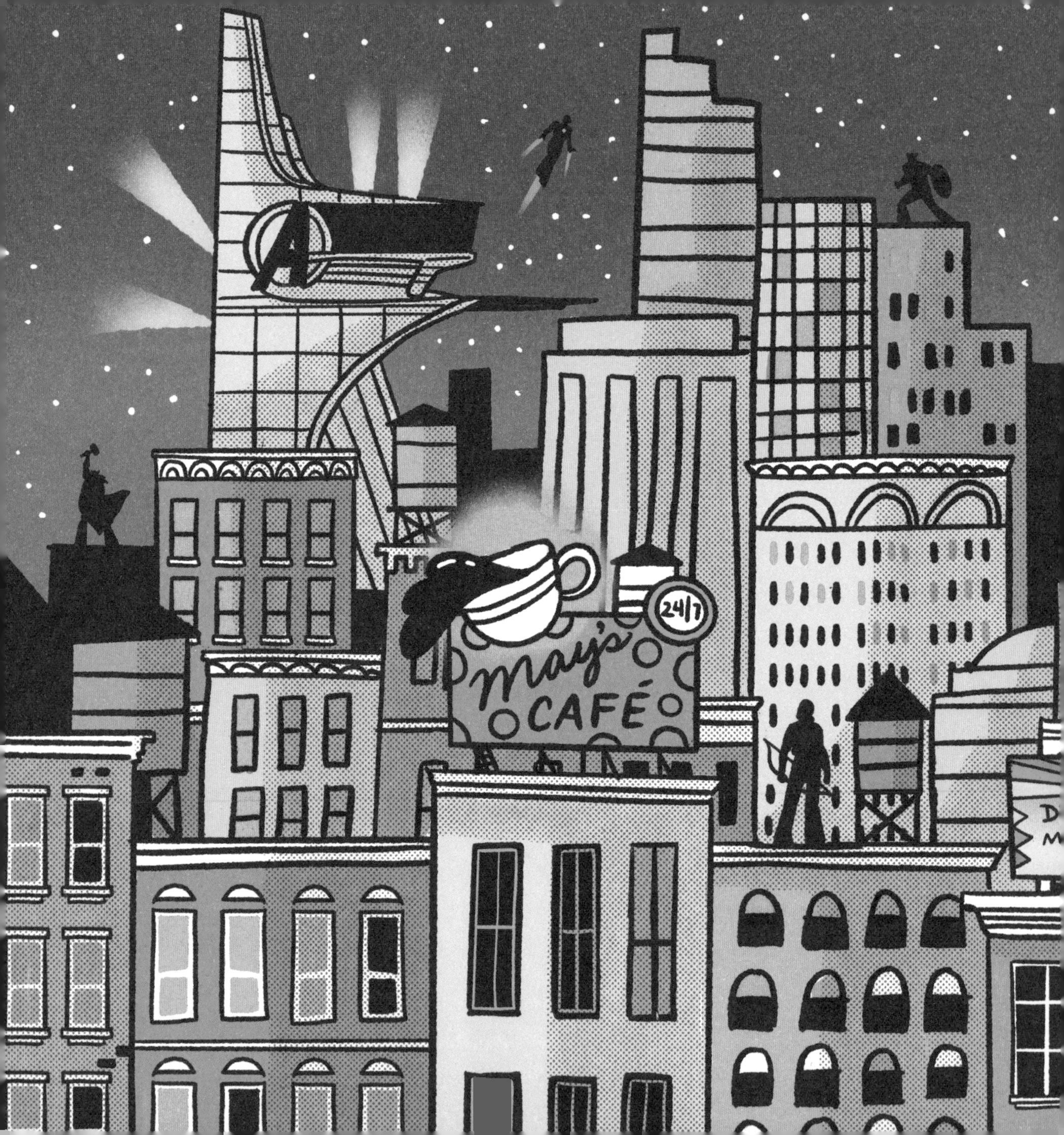
24/7
may's
CAFÉ